Tiny Tyrant

Volume Two: The Lucky Winner

Translated by Alexis Siegel
Color by Fabrice Parme & Véronique Dreher

:01
First Second
New York & London

Contents

A Surprise Visit

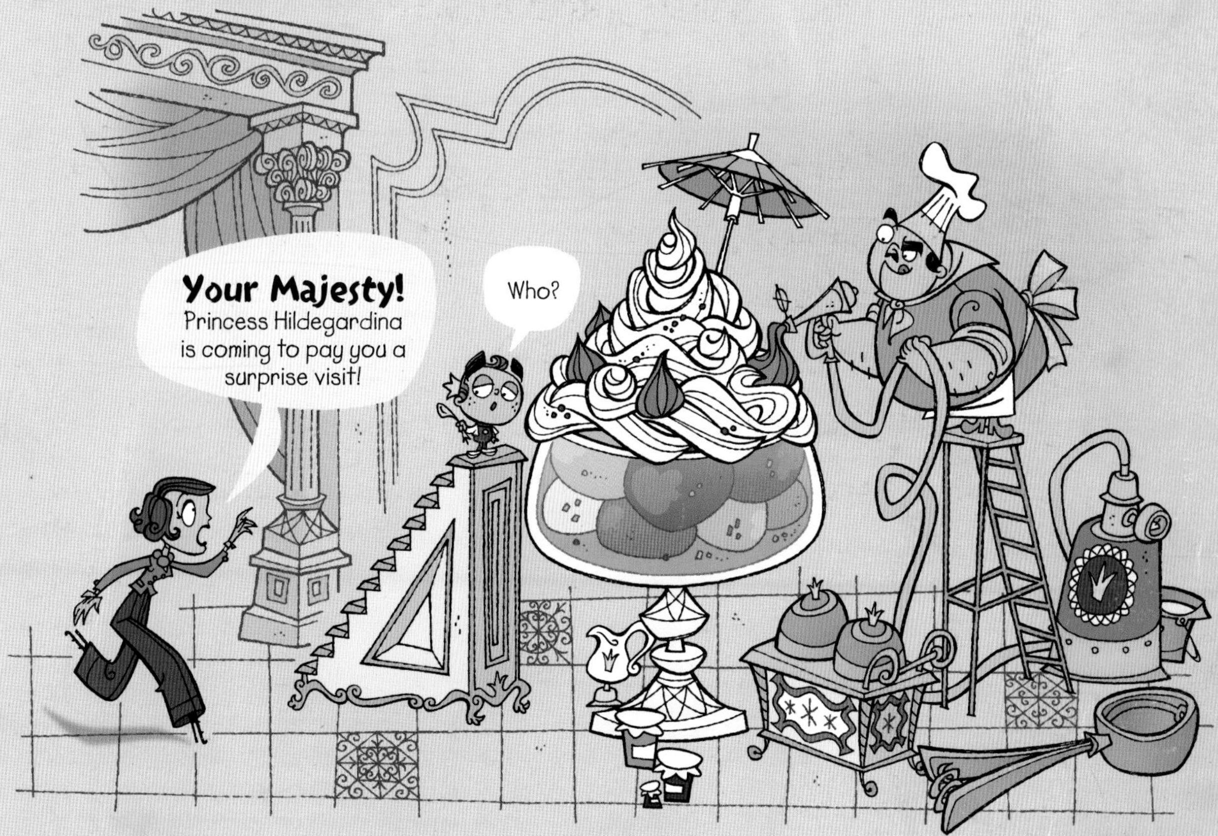
Your Majesty! Princess Hildegardina is coming to pay you a surprise visit!
Who?

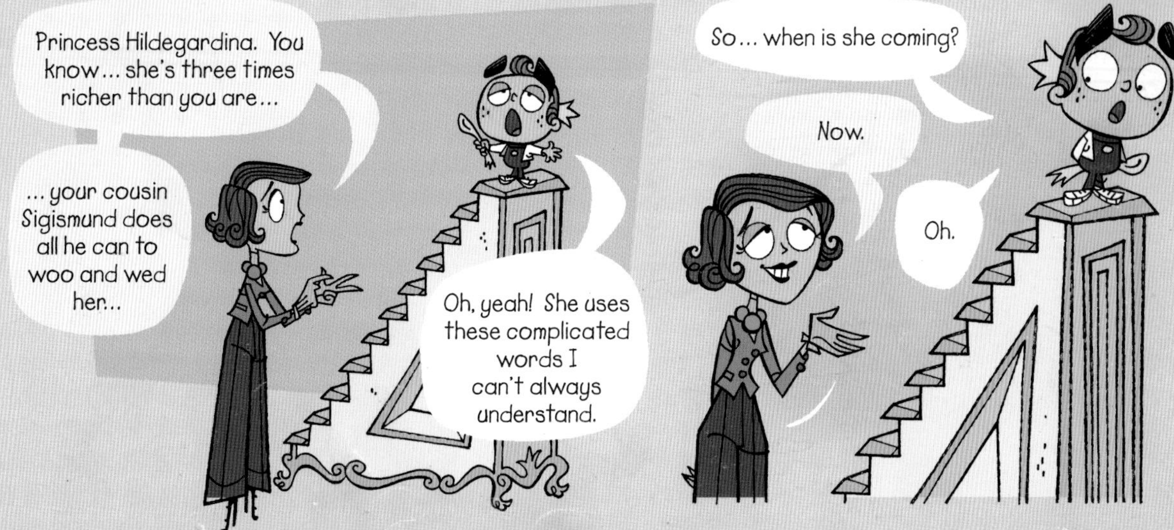
Princess Hildegardina. You know... she's three times richer than you are...
... your cousin Sigismund does all he can to woo and wed her...
Oh, yeah! She uses these complicated words I can't always understand.
So... when is she coming?
Now.
Oh.

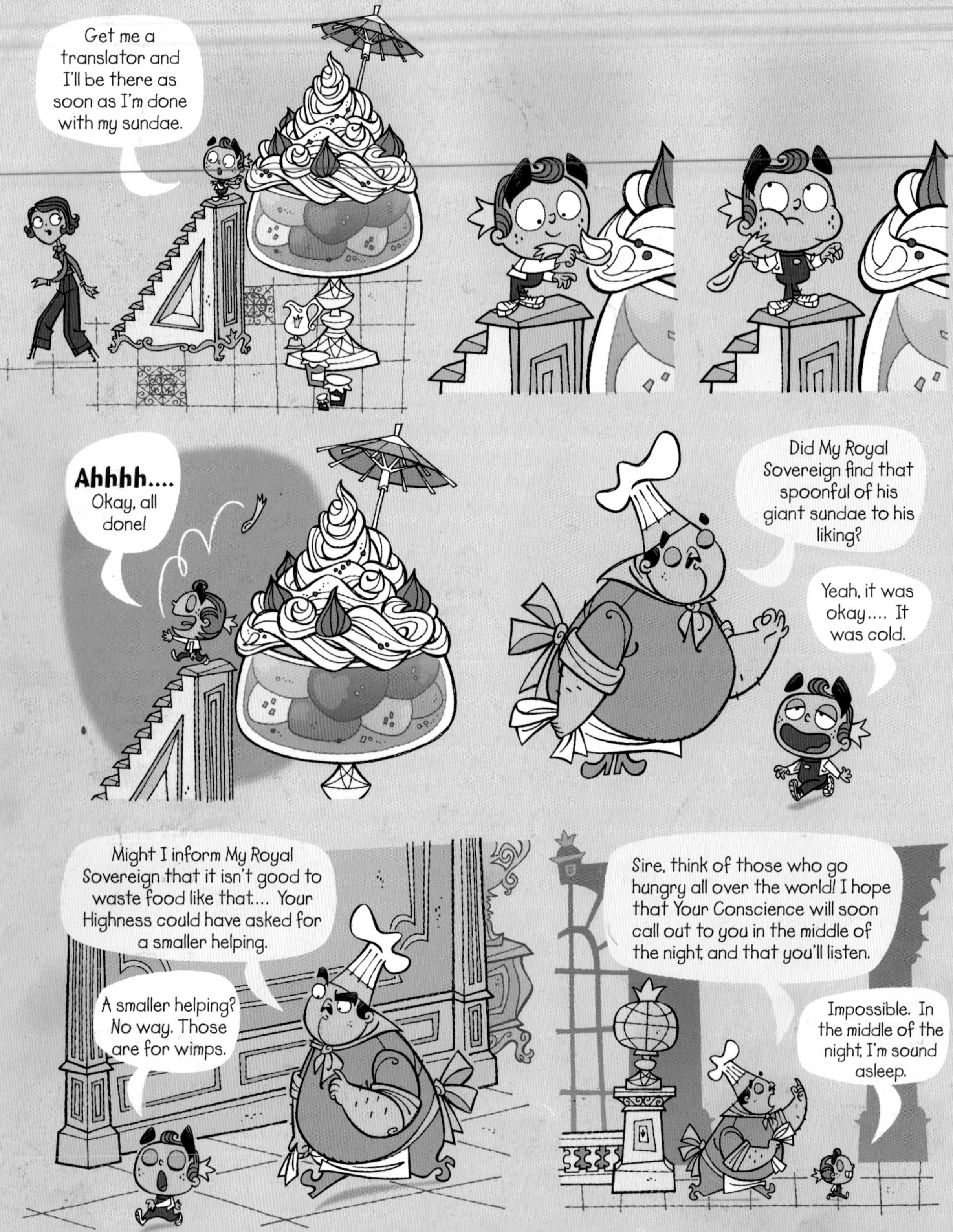
Get me a translator and I'll be there as soon as I'm done with my sundae.
Ahhhh.... Okay, all done!
Did My Royal Sovereign find that spoonful of his giant sundae to his liking?
Yeah, it was okay.... It was cold.
Might I inform My Royal Sovereign that it isn't good to waste food like that.... Your Highness could have asked for a smaller helping.
A smaller helping? No way. Those are for wimps.
Sire, think of those who go hungry all over the world! I hope that Your Conscience will soon call out to you in the middle of the night, and that you'll listen.
Impossible. In the middle of the night, I'm sound asleep.

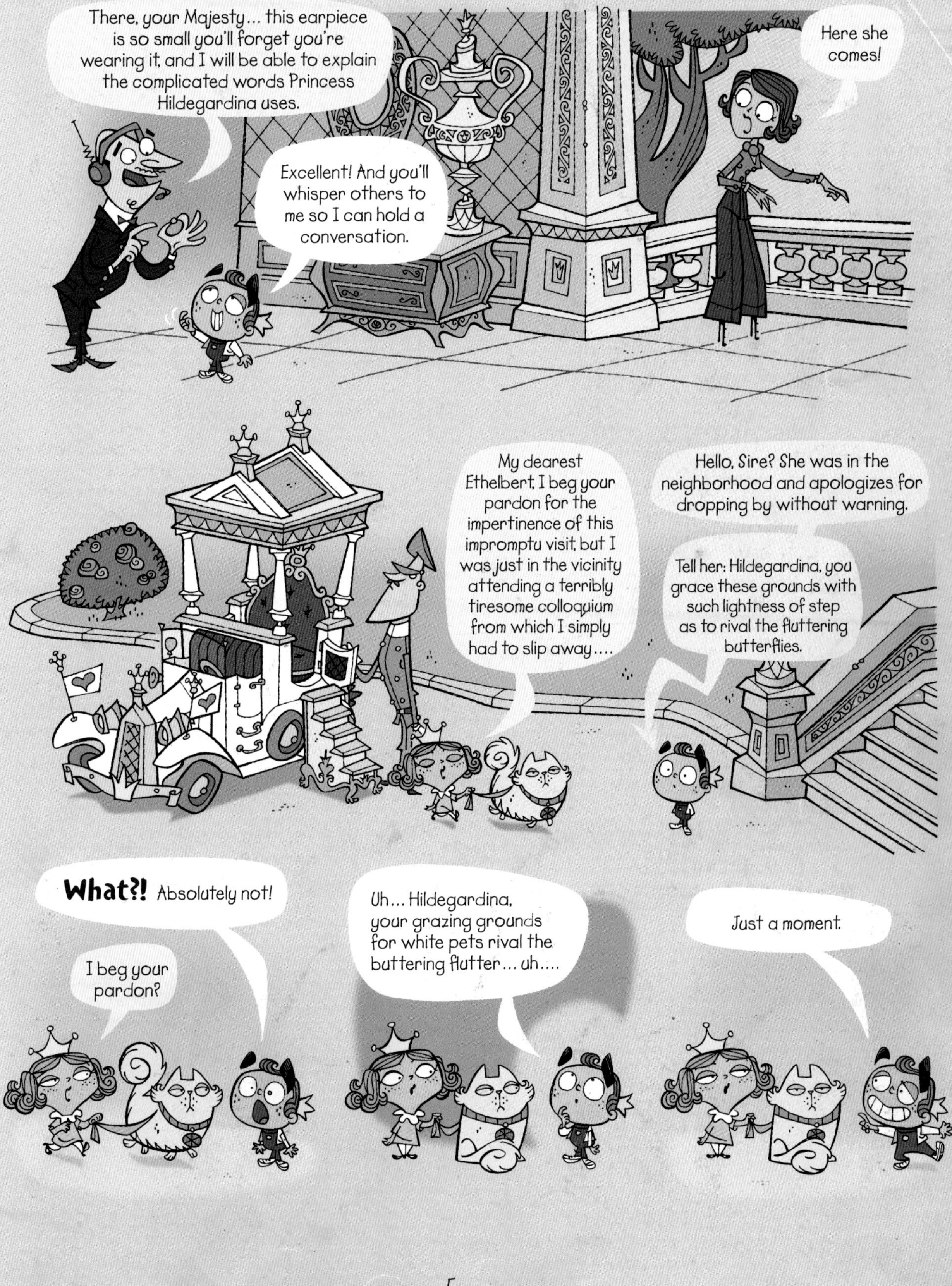
There, your Majesty... this earpiece is so small you'll forget you're wearing it, and I will be able to explain the complicated words Princess Hildegardina uses.
Excellent! And you'll whisper others to me so I can hold a conversation.
Here she comes!
My dearest Ethelbert, I beg your pardon for the impertinence of this impromptu visit, but I was just in the vicinity attending a terribly tiresome colloquium from which I simply had to slip away....
Hello, Sire? She was in the neighborhood and apologizes for dropping by without warning.
Tell her: Hildegardina, you grace these grounds with such lightness of step as to rival the fluttering butterflies.
What?! Absolutely not!
I beg your pardon?
Uh... Hildegardina, your grazing grounds for white pets rival the buttering flutter... uh....
Just a moment.

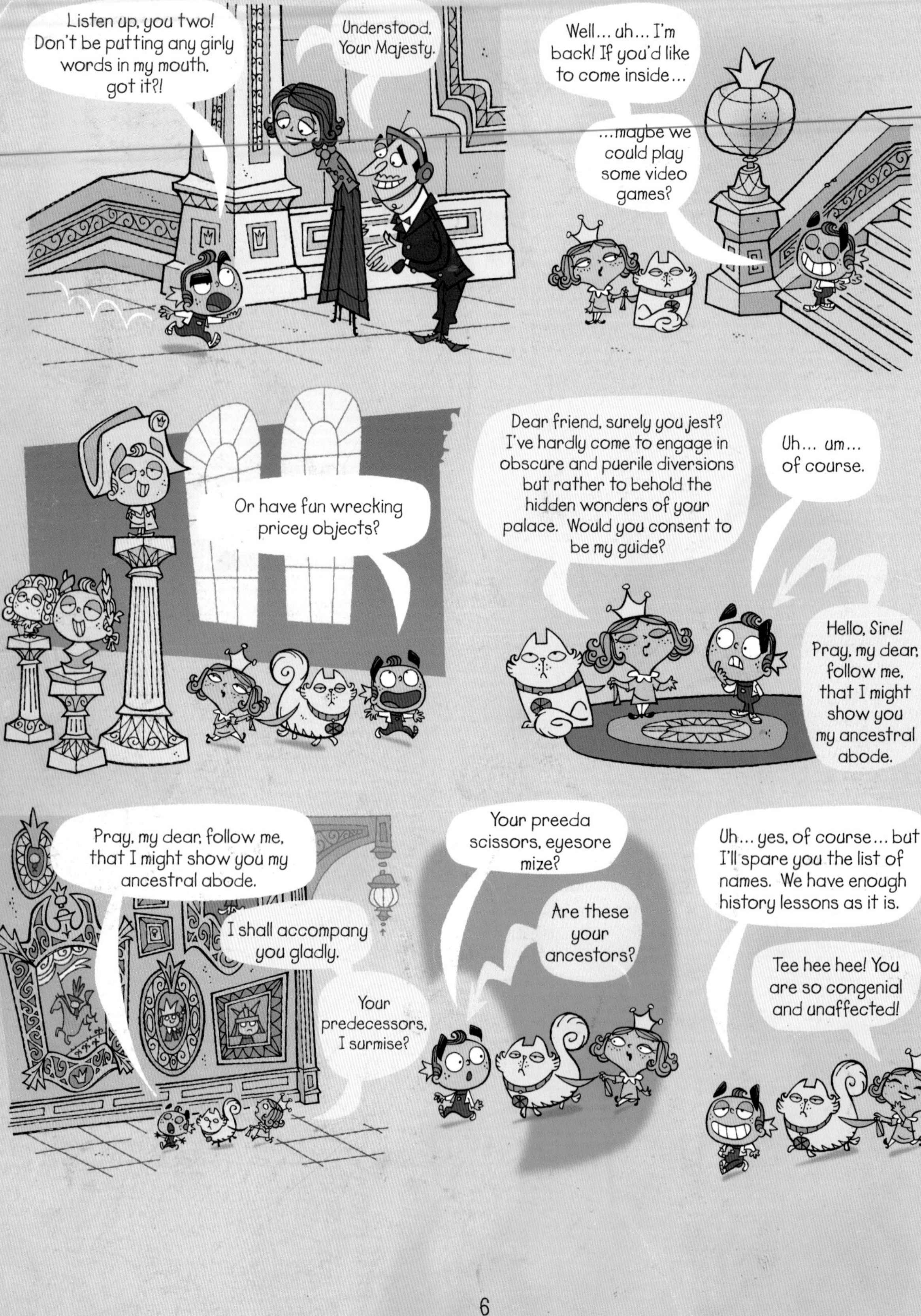

Listen up, you two! Don't be putting any girly words in my mouth, got it?!
Understood, Your Majesty.
Well... uh... I'm back! If you'd like to come inside...
...maybe we could play some video games?
Or have fun wrecking pricey objects?
Dear friend, surely you jest? I've hardly come to engage in obscure and puerile diversions but rather to behold the hidden wonders of your palace. Would you consent to be my guide?
Uh... um... of course.
Hello, Sire! Pray, my dear, follow me, that I might show you my ancestral abode.
Pray, my dear, follow me, that I might show you my ancestral abode.
I shall accompany you gladly.
Your predecessors, I surmise?
Your preeda scissors, eyesore mize?
Are these your ancestors?
Uh... yes, of course... but I'll spare you the list of names. We have enough history lessons as it is.
Tee hee hee! You are so congenial and unaffected!

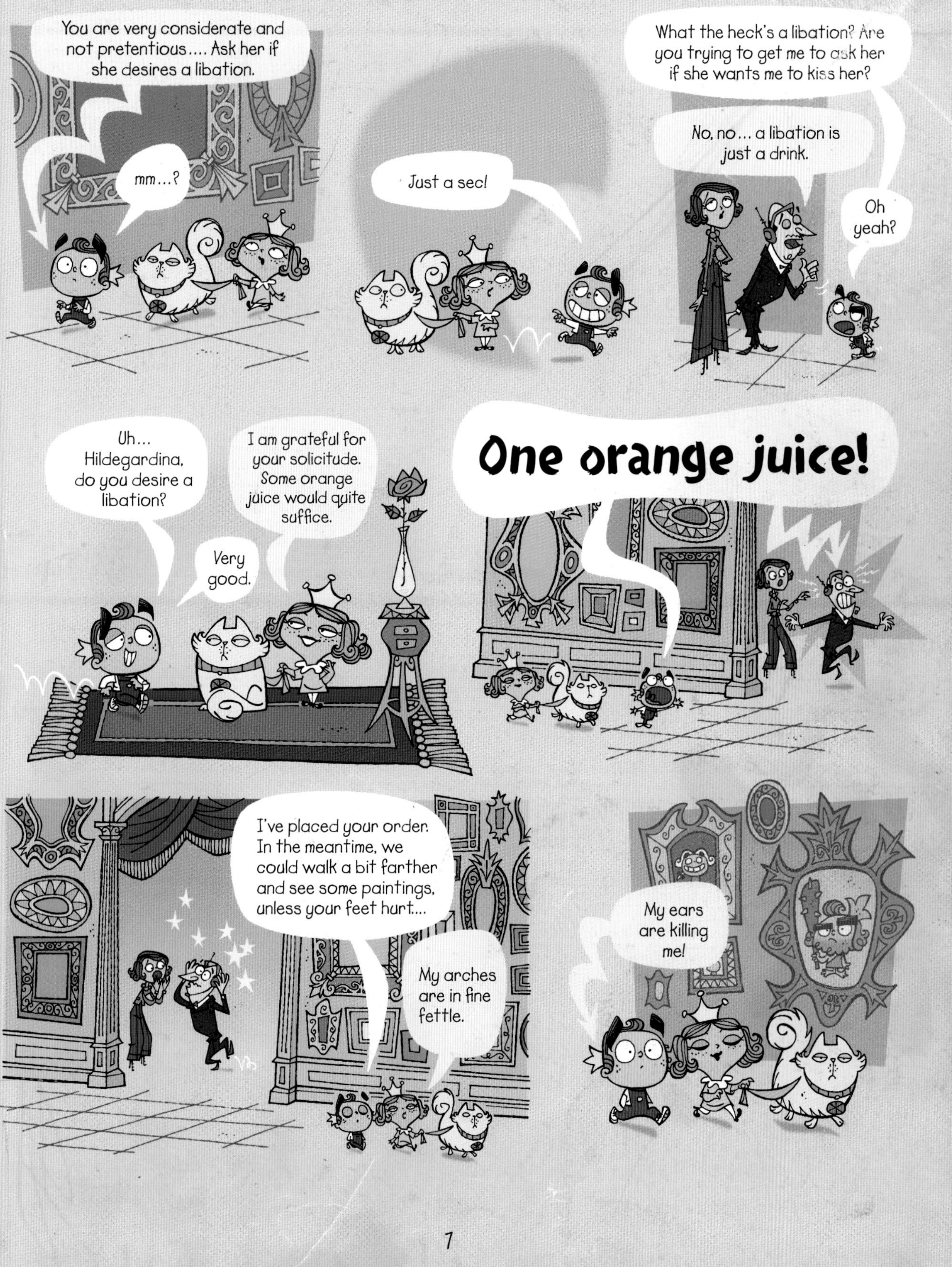
You are very considerate and not pretentious.... Ask her if she desires a libation.
mm...?
Just a sec!
What the heck's a libation? Are you trying to get me to ask her if she wants me to kiss her?
No, no... a libation is just a drink.
Oh yeah?
Uh... Hildegardina, do you desire a libation?
Very good.
I am grateful for your solicitude. Some orange juice would quite suffice.
One orange juice!
I've placed your order. In the meantime, we could walk a bit farther and see some paintings, unless your feet hurt....
My arches are in fine fettle.
My ears are killing me!

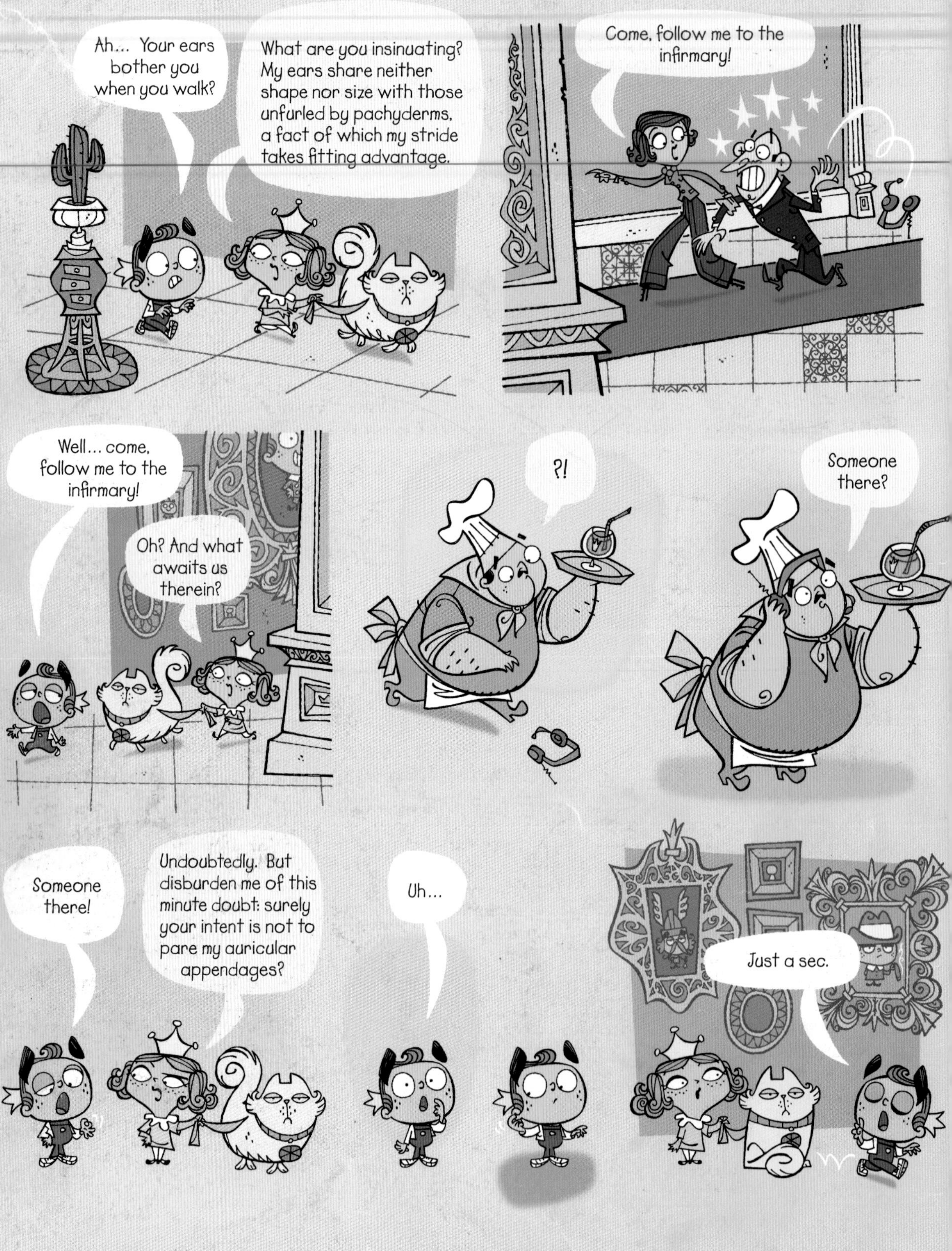
Ah... Your ears bother you when you walk?
What are you insinuating? My ears share neither shape nor size with those unfurled by pachyderms, a fact of which my stride takes fitting advantage.
Come, follow me to the infirmary!
Well... come, follow me to the infirmary!
Oh? And what awaits us therein?
?!
Someone there?
Someone there!
Undoubtedly. But disburden me of this minute doubt: surely your intent is not to pare my auricular appendages?
Uh...
Just a sec.

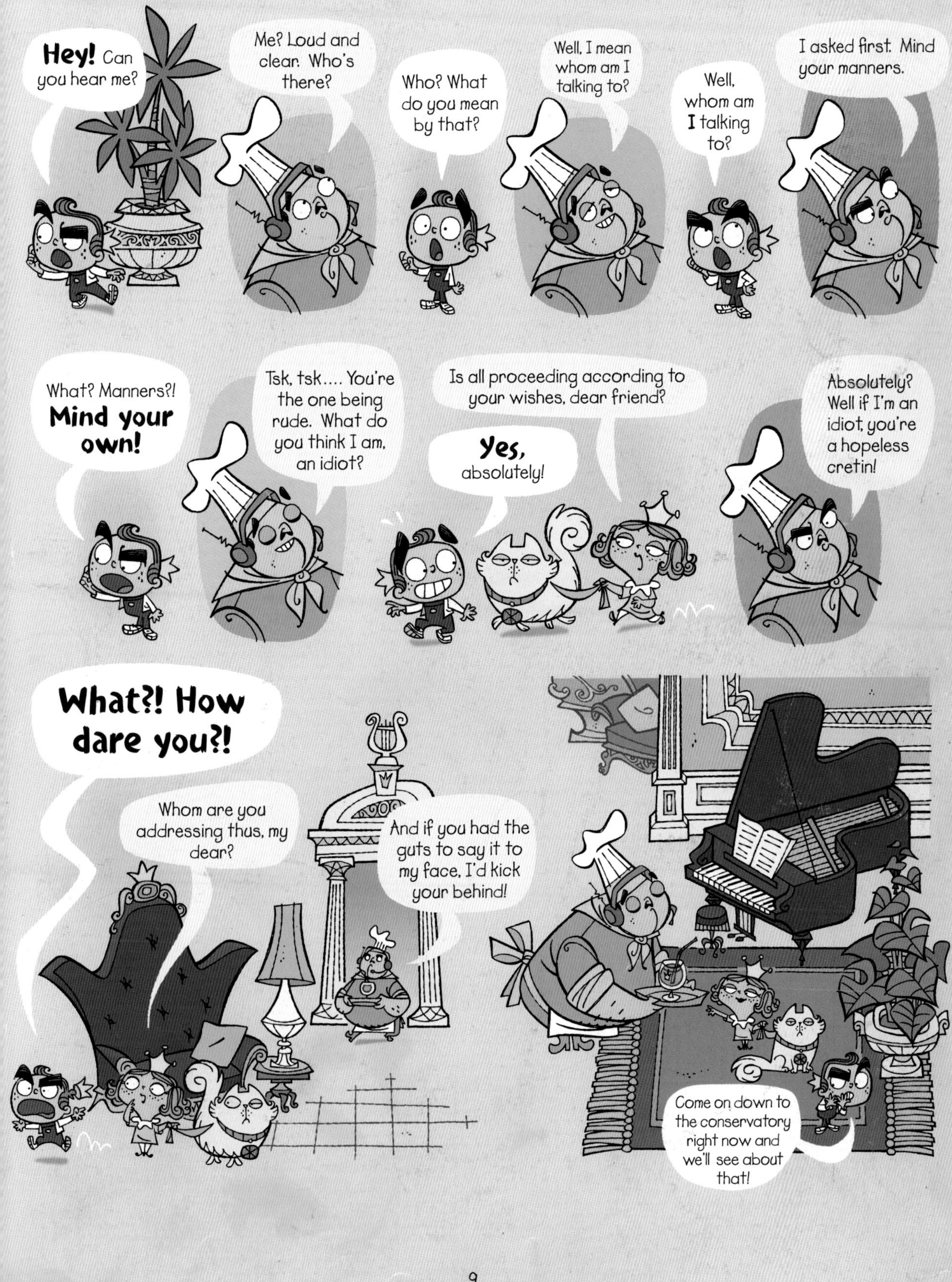

Hey! Can you hear me?
Me? Loud and clear. Who's there?
Who? What do you mean by that?
Well, I mean whom am I talking to?
Well, whom am I talking to?
I asked first. Mind your manners.
What? Manners?! Mind your own!
Tsk, tsk.... You're the one being rude. What do you think I am, an idiot?
Is all proceeding according to your wishes, dear friend?
Yes, absolutely!
Absolutely? Well if I'm an idiot, you're a hopeless cretin!
What?! How dare you?!
Whom are you addressing thus, my dear?
And if you had the guts to say it to my face, I'd kick your behind!
Come on down to the conservatory right now and we'll see about that!

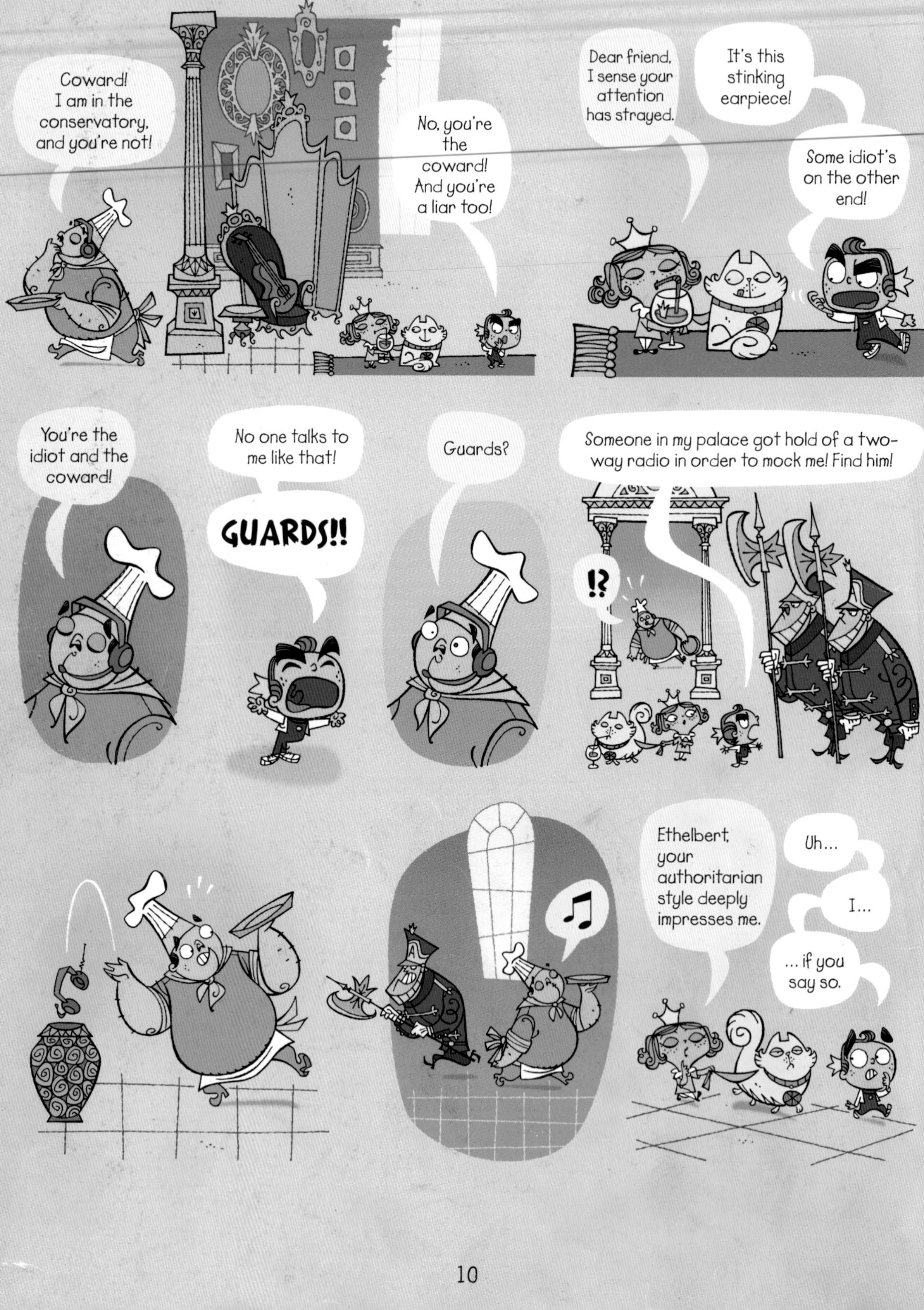
Coward! I am in the conservatory, and you're not!
No, you're the coward! And you're a liar too!
Dear friend, I sense your attention has strayed.
It's this stinking earpiece!
Some idiot's on the other end!
You're the idiot and the coward!
No one talks to me like that!
GUARDS!!
Guards?
Someone in my palace got hold of a two-way radio in order to mock me! Find him!
!?
Ethelbert, your authoritarian style deeply impresses me.
Uh...
I...
... if you say so.

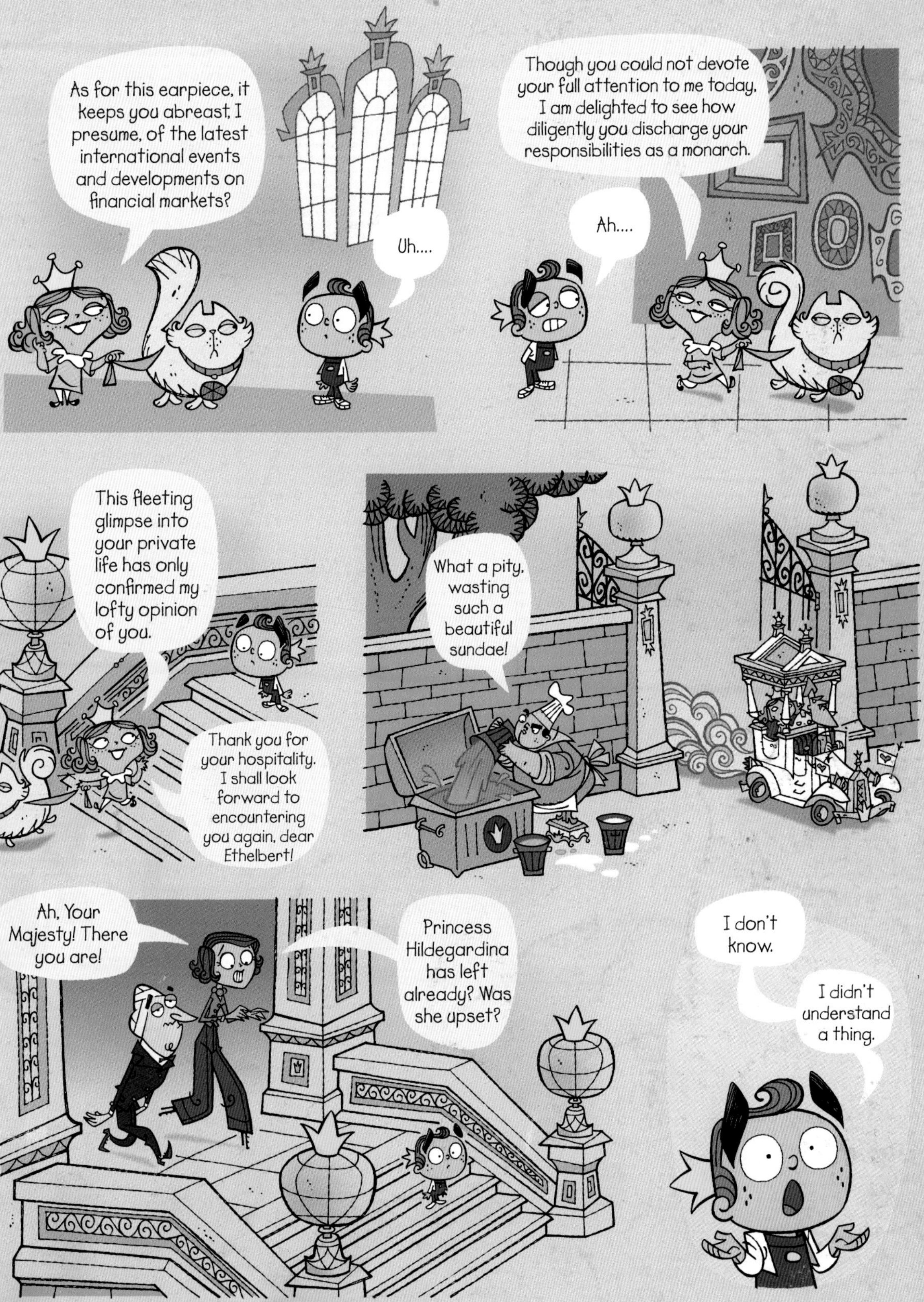

As for this earpiece, it keeps you abreast, I presume, of the latest international events and developments on financial markets?
Uh....
Though you could not devote your full attention to me today, I am delighted to see how diligently you discharge your responsibilities as a monarch.
Ah....
This fleeting glimpse into your private life has only confirmed my lofty opinion of you.
Thank you for your hospitality. I shall look forward to encountering you again, dear Ethelbert!
What a pity, wasting such a beautiful sundae!
Ah, Your Majesty! There you are!
Princess Hildegardina has left already? Was she upset?
I don't know.
I didn't understand a thing.

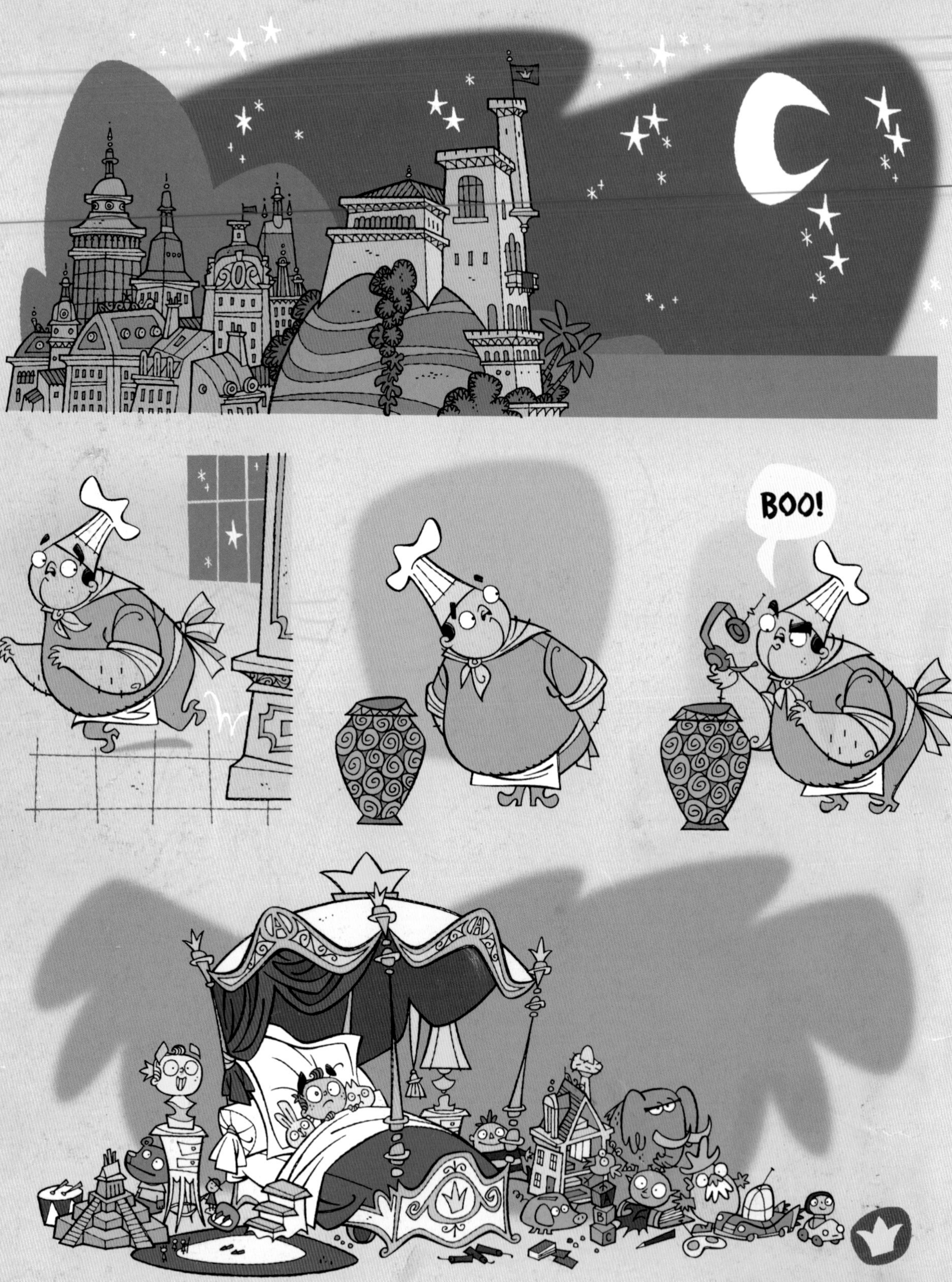
BOO!

The Lucky Winner

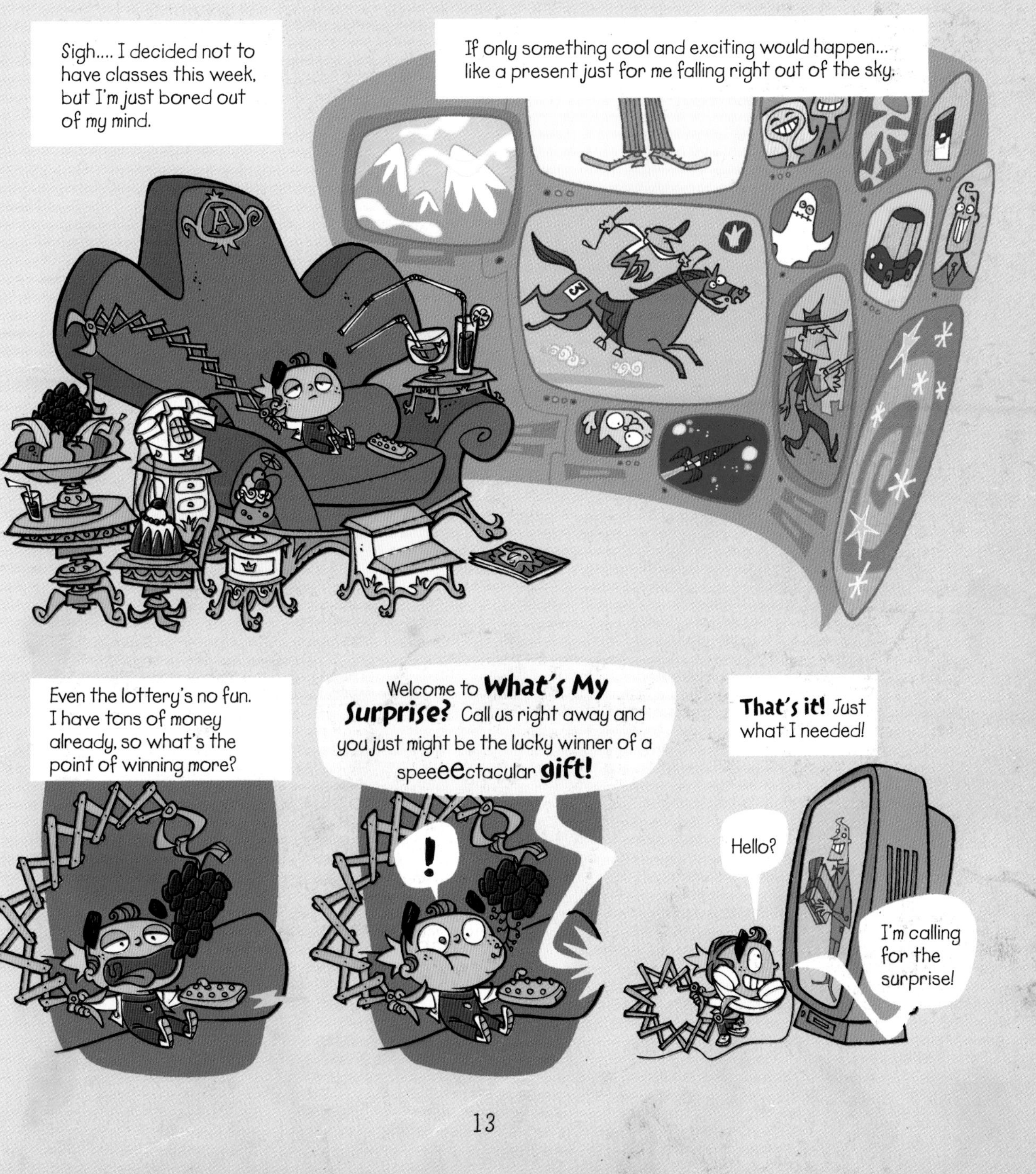

Sigh.... I decided not to have classes this week, but I'm just bored out of my mind.
If only something cool and exciting would happen... like a present just for me falling right out of the sky.
Even the lottery's no fun. I have tons of money already, so what's the point of winning more?
Welcome to What's My Surprise? Call us right away and you just might be the lucky winner of a speeeeectacular gift!
!
That's it! Just what I needed!
Hello?
I'm calling for the surprise!

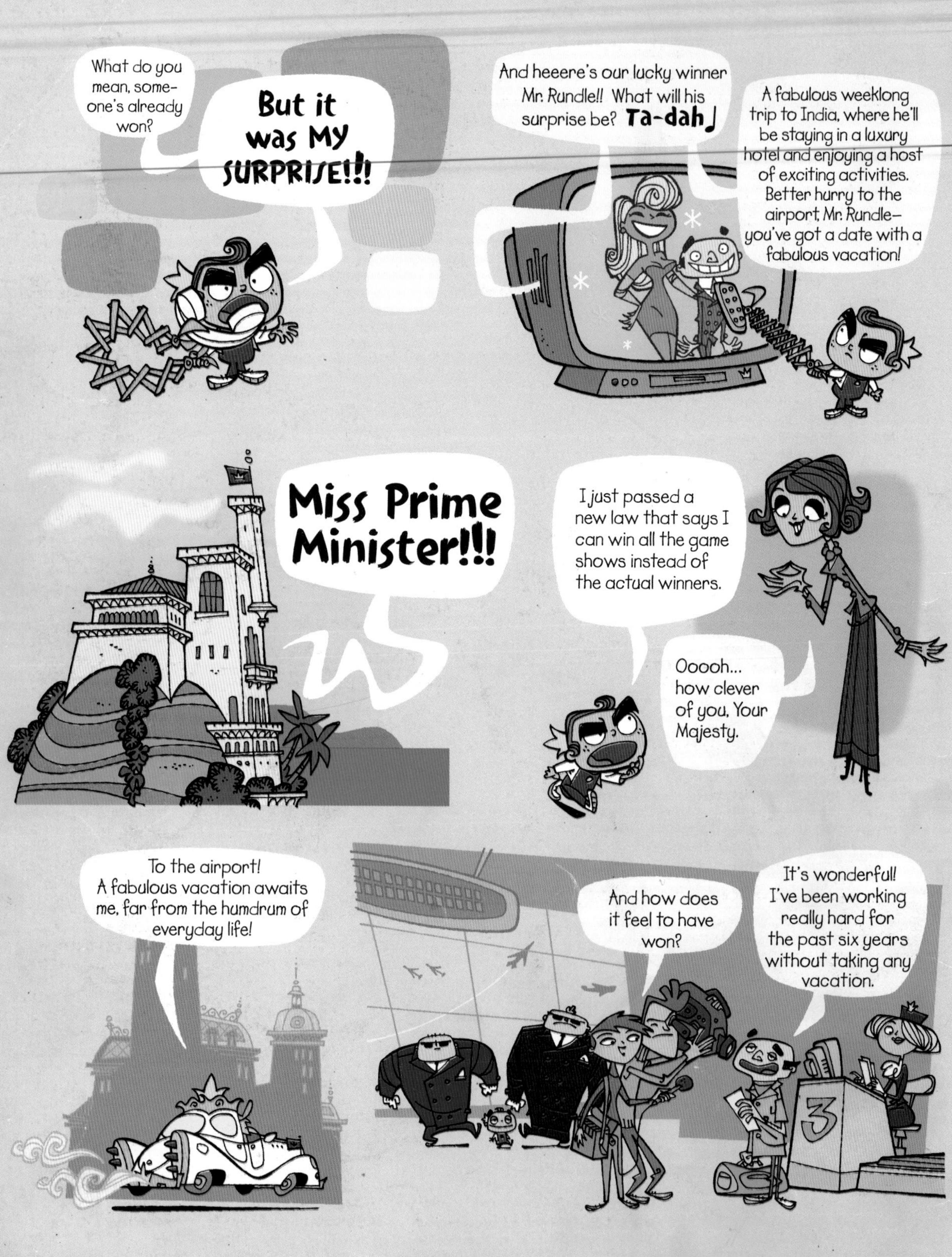
What do you mean, someone's already won?
But it was MY SURPRISE!!!
And heeere's our lucky winner Mr. Rundle!! What will his surprise be? Ta-dah♩
A fabulous weeklong trip to India, where he'll be staying in a luxury hotel and enjoying a host of exciting activities. Better hurry to the airport, Mr. Rundle— you've got a date with a fabulous vacation!
Miss Prime Minister!!!
I just passed a new law that says I can win all the game shows instead of the actual winners.
Ooooh... how clever of you, Your Majesty.
To the airport! A fabulous vacation awaits me, far from the humdrum of everyday life!
And how does it feel to have won?
It's wonderful! I've been working really hard for the past six years without taking any vacation.
3

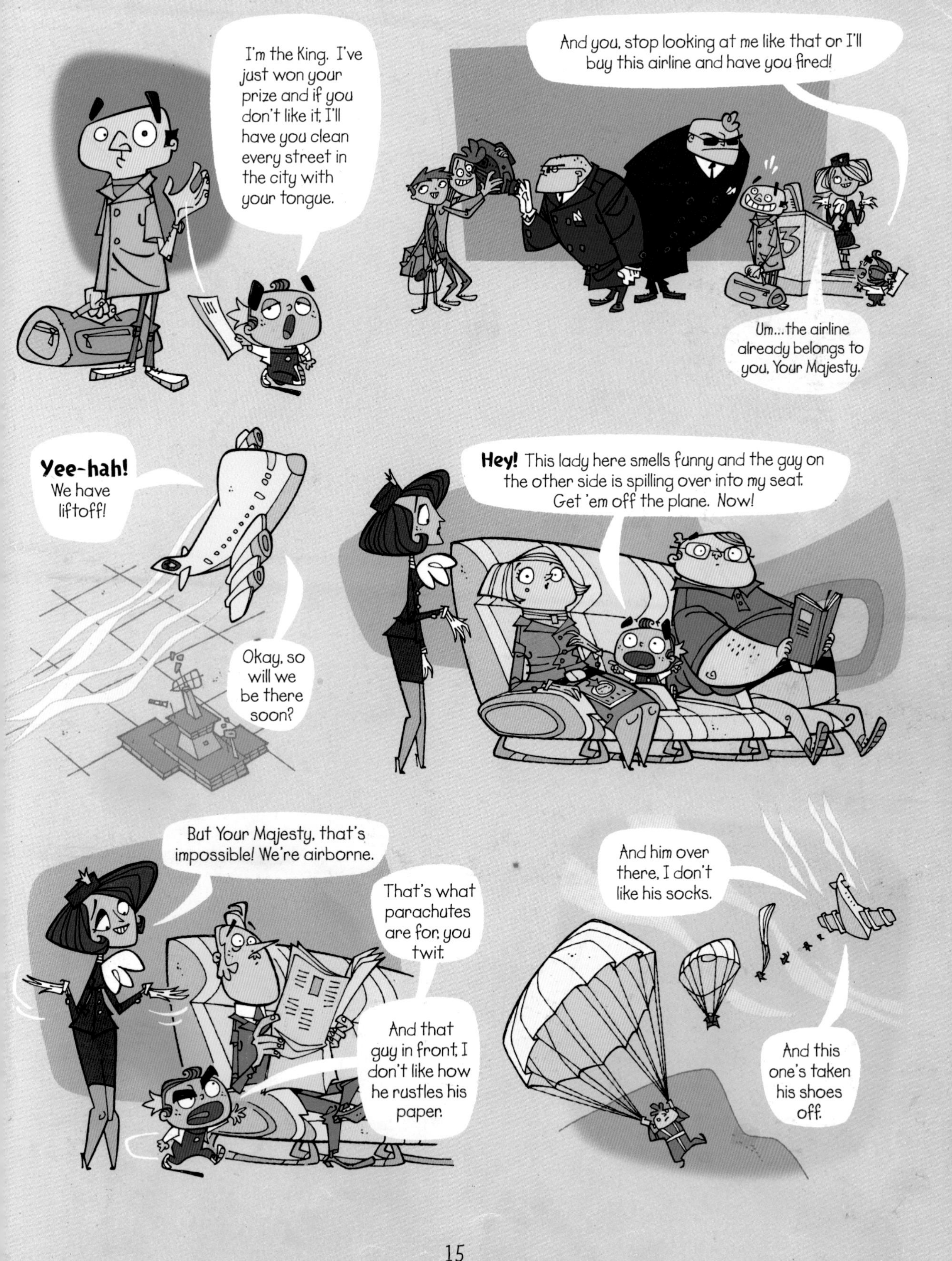
I'm the King. I've just won your prize and if you don't like it, I'll have you clean every street in the city with your tongue.
And you, stop looking at me like that or I'll buy this airline and have you fired!
Um...the airline already belongs to you, Your Majesty.
Yee-hah! We have liftoff!
Okay, so will we be there soon?
Hey! This lady here smells funny and the guy on the other side is spilling over into my seat. Get 'em off the plane. Now!
But Your Majesty, that's impossible! We're airborne.
That's what parachutes are for, you twit.
And that guy in front, I don't like how he rustles his paper.
And him over there, I don't like his socks.
And this one's taken his shoes off.

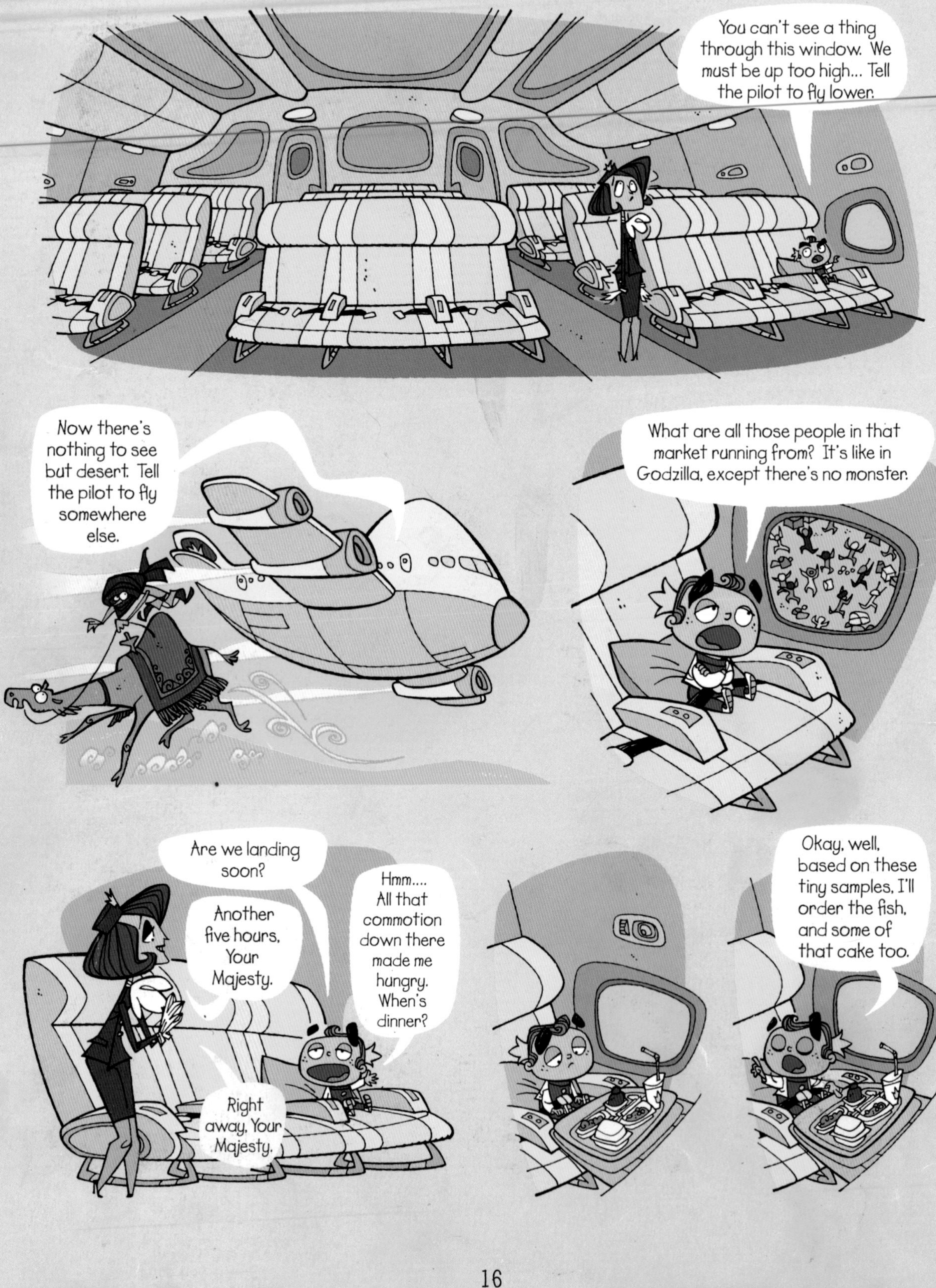

You can't see a thing through this window. We must be up too high... Tell the pilot to fly lower.
Now there's nothing to see but desert. Tell the pilot to fly somewhere else.
What are all those people in that market running from? It's like in Godzilla, except there's no monster.
Are we landing soon?
Another five hours, Your Majesty.
Hmm.... All that commotion down there made me hungry. When's dinner?
Right away, Your Majesty.
Okay, well, based on these tiny samples, I'll order the fish, and some of that cake too.

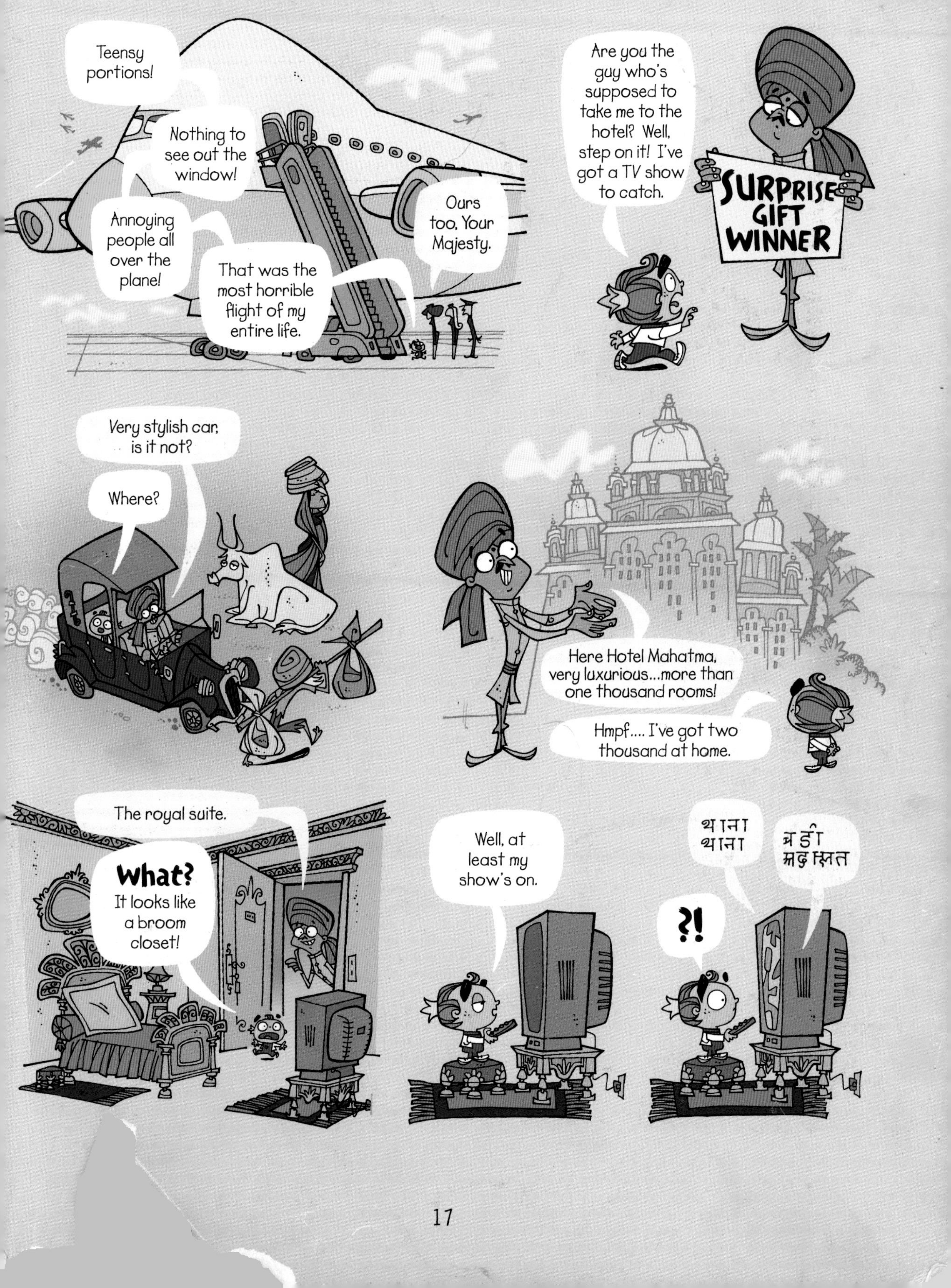
Teensy portions!
Nothing to see out the window!
Annoying people all over the plane!
That was the most horrible flight of my entire life.
Ours too, Your Majesty.
Are you the guy who's supposed to take me to the hotel? Well, step on it! I've got a TV show to catch.
SURPRISE GIFT WINNER
Very stylish car, is it not?
Where?
Here Hotel Mahatma, very luxurious...more than one thousand rooms!
Hmpf.... I've got two thousand at home.
The royal suite.
What? It looks like a broom closet!
Well, at least my show's on.
?!
थाना थाना

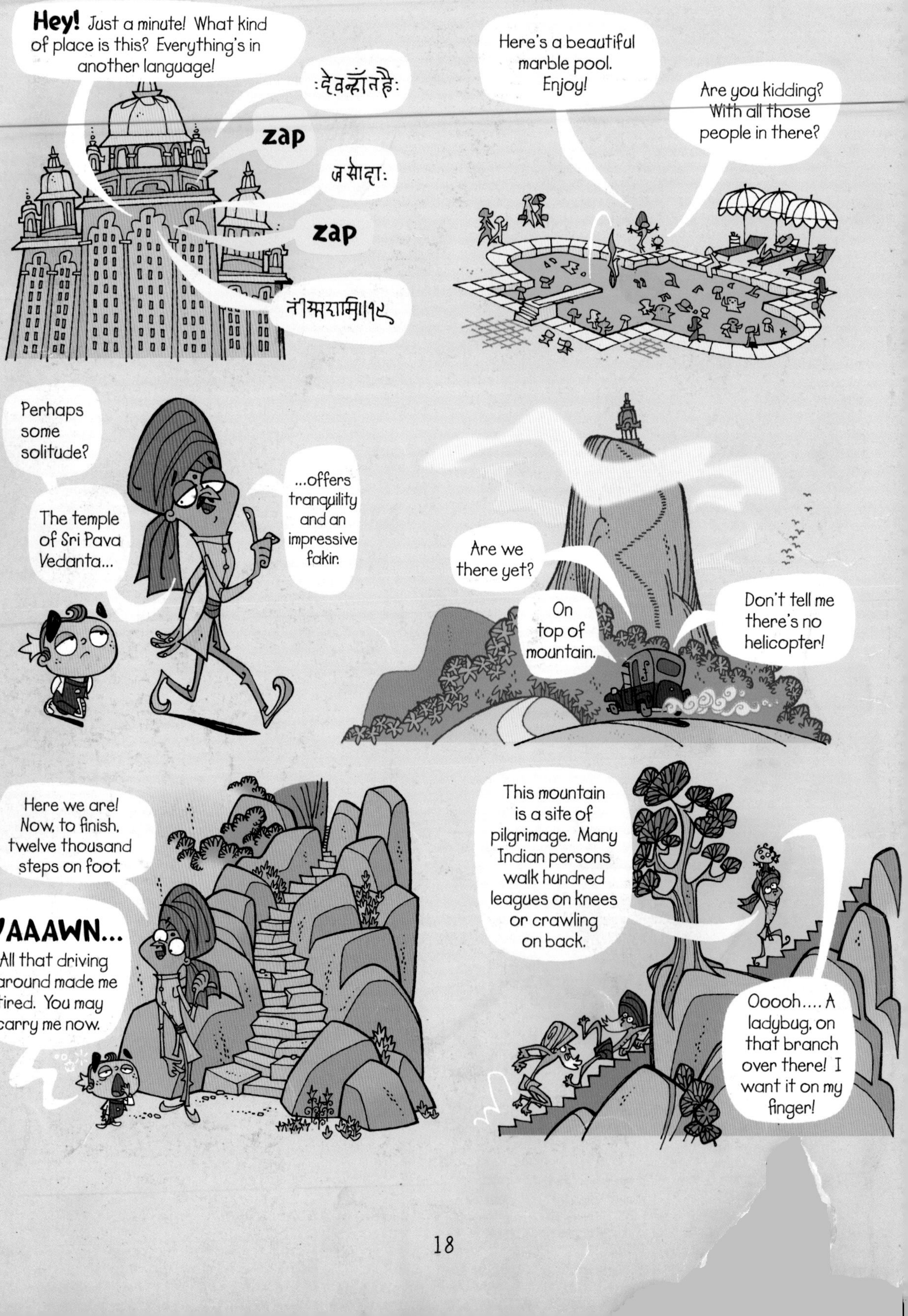

Hey! Just a minute! What kind of place is this? Everything's in another language!
zap
zap
Here's a beautiful marble pool. Enjoy!
Are you kidding? With all those people in there?
Perhaps some solitude?
The temple of Sri Pava Vedanta...
...offers tranquility and an impressive fakir.
Are we there yet?
On top of mountain.
Don't tell me there's no helicopter!
Here we are! Now, to finish, twelve thousand steps on foot.
YAAAWN...
All that driving around made me tired. You may carry me now.
This mountain is a site of pilgrimage. Many Indian persons walk hundred leagues on knees or crawling on back.
Ooooh.... A ladybug, on that branch over there! I want it on my finger!

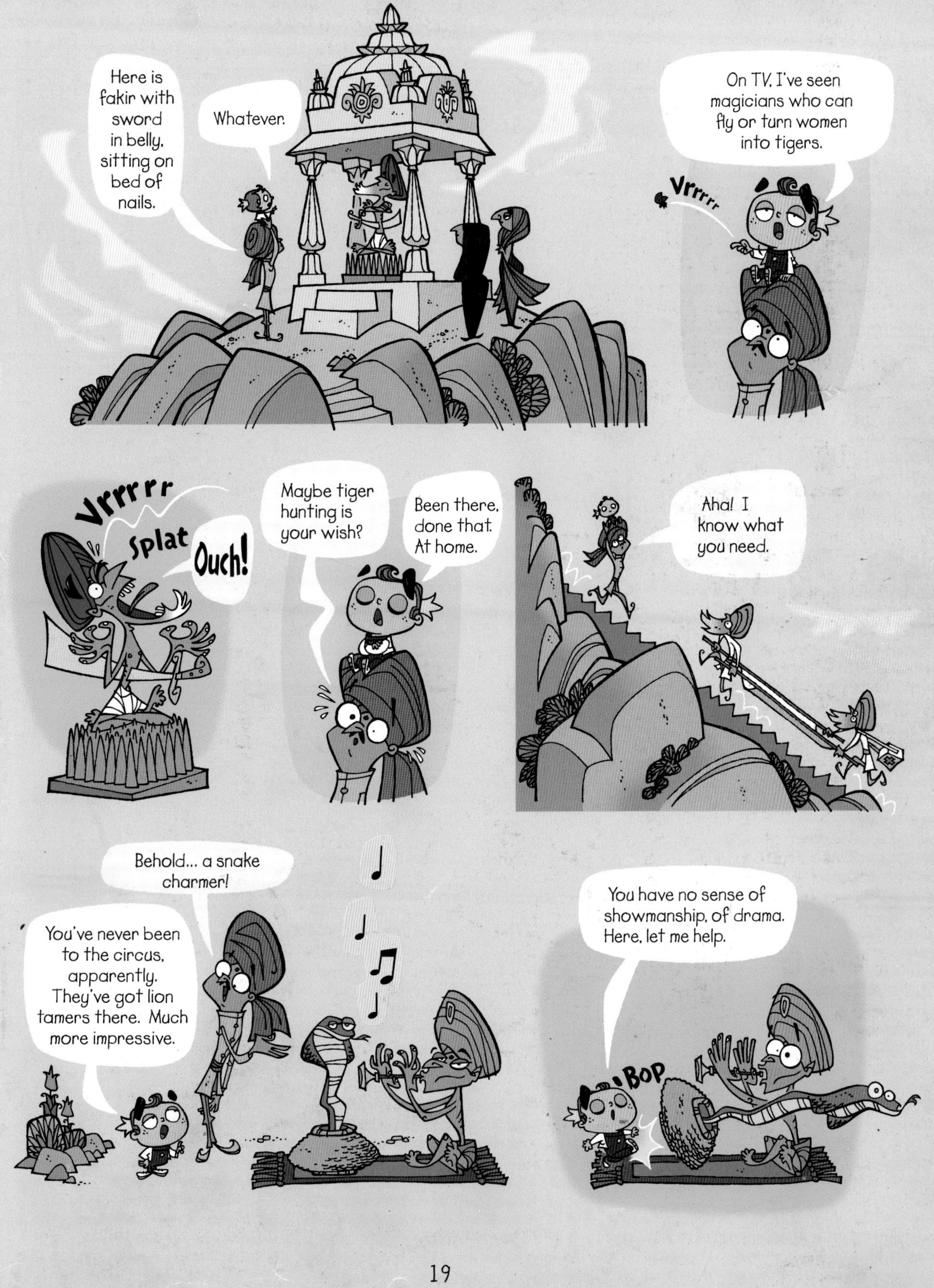

Here is fakir with sword in belly, sitting on bed of nails.
Whatever.
On TV, I've seen magicians who can fly or turn women into tigers.
Vrrrrr
Vrrrrr
Splat
Ouch!
Maybe tiger hunting is your wish?
Been there, done that. At home.
Aha! I know what you need.
Behold... a snake charmer!
You've never been to the circus, apparently. They've got lion tamers there. Much more impressive.
You have no sense of showmanship, of drama. Here, let me help.
BOP

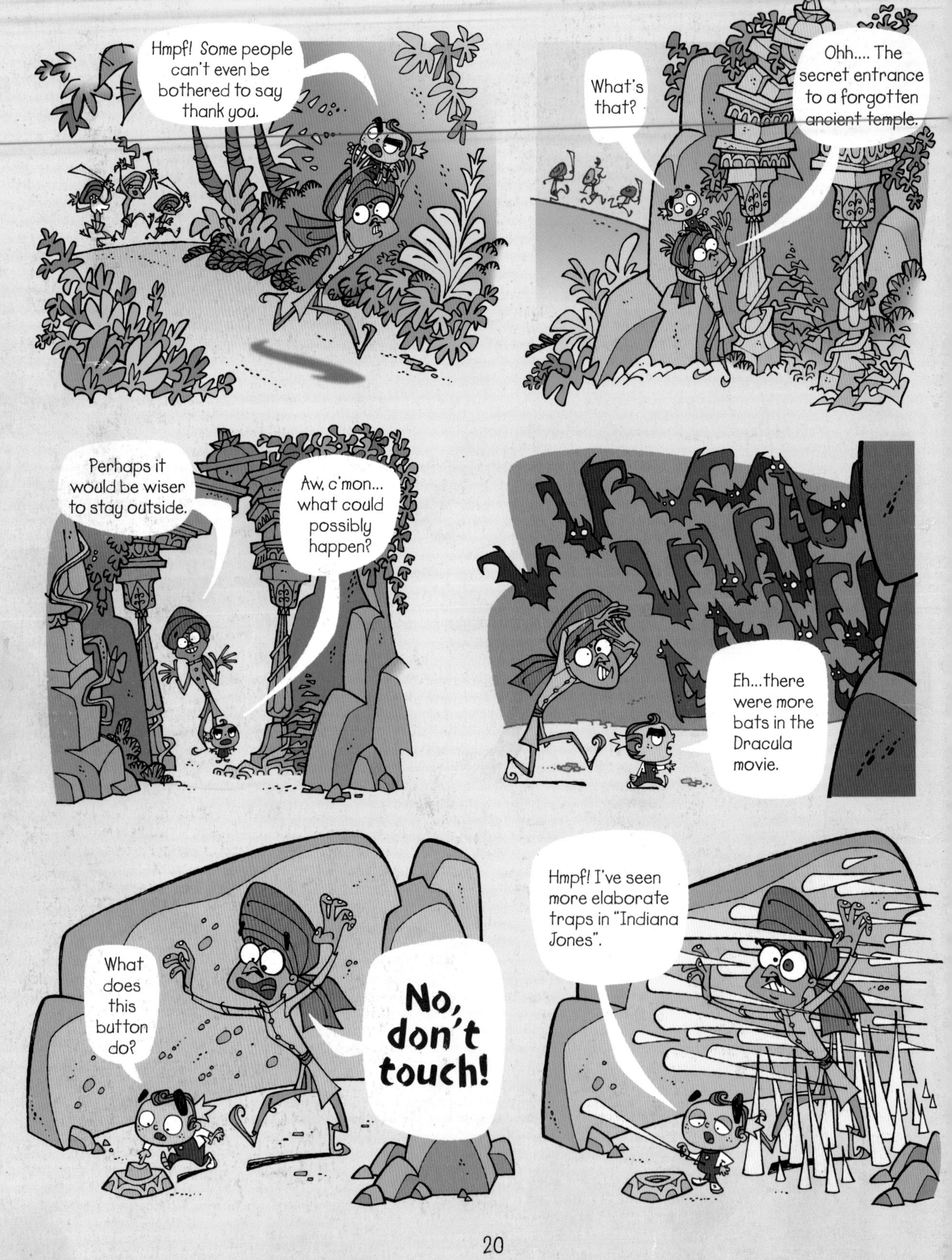
Hmpf! Some people can't even be bothered to say thank you.
What's that?
Ohh.... The secret entrance to a forgotten ancient temple.
Perhaps it would be wiser to stay outside.
Aw, c'mon... what could possibly happen?
Eh...there were more bats in the Dracula movie.
What does this button do?
No, don't touch!
Hmpf! I've seen more elaborate traps in "Indiana Jones".

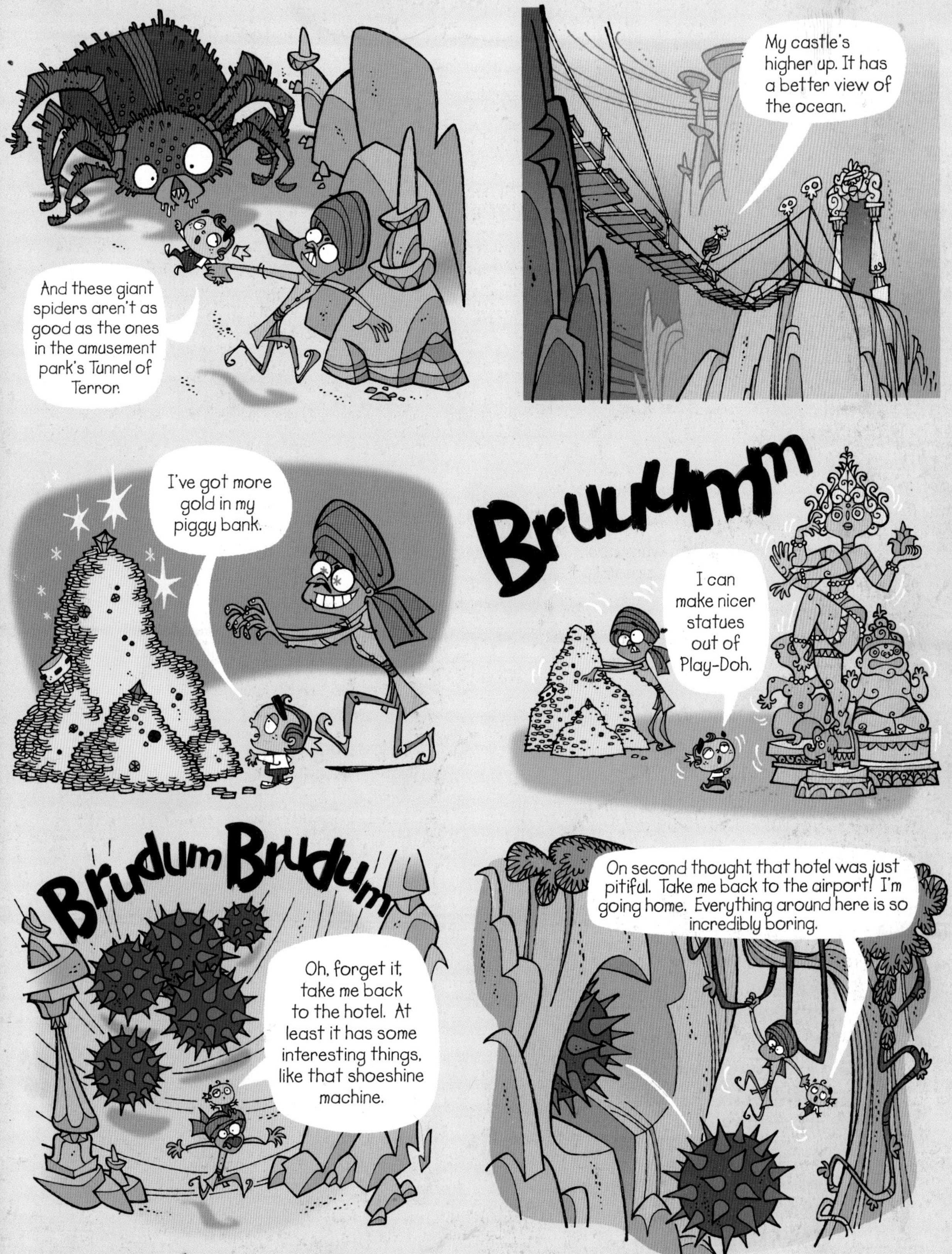
And these giant spiders aren't as good as the ones in the amusement park's Tunnel of Terror.
My castle's higher up. It has a better view of the ocean.
I've got more gold in my piggy bank.
Bruuumm
I can make nicer statues out of Play-Doh.
Brudum Brudum
Oh, forget it, take me back to the hotel. At least it has some interesting things, like that shoeshine machine.
On second thought, that hotel was just pitiful. Take me back to the airport! I'm going home. Everything around here is so incredibly boring.

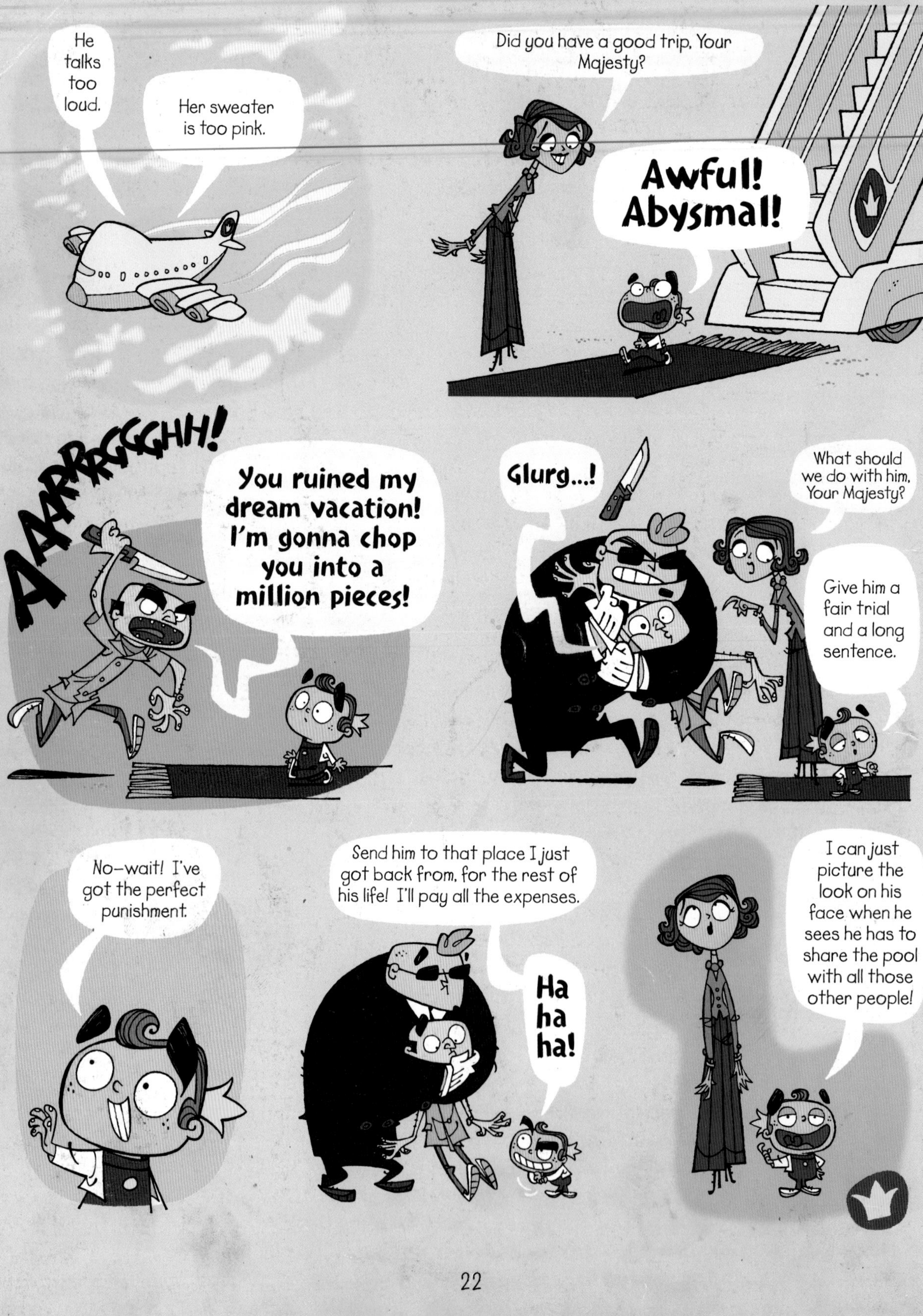
He talks too loud.
Her sweater is too pink.
Did you have a good trip, Your Majesty?
Awful! Abysmal!
AARRRGGGHH!
You ruined my dream vacation! I'm gonna chop you into a million pieces!
Glurg...!
What should we do with him, Your Majesty?
Give him a fair trial and a long sentence.
No–wait! I've got the perfect punishment.
Send him to that place I just got back from, for the rest of his life! I'll pay all the expenses.
Ha ha ha!
I can just picture the look on his face when he sees he has to share the pool with all those other people!

A Routine Investigation

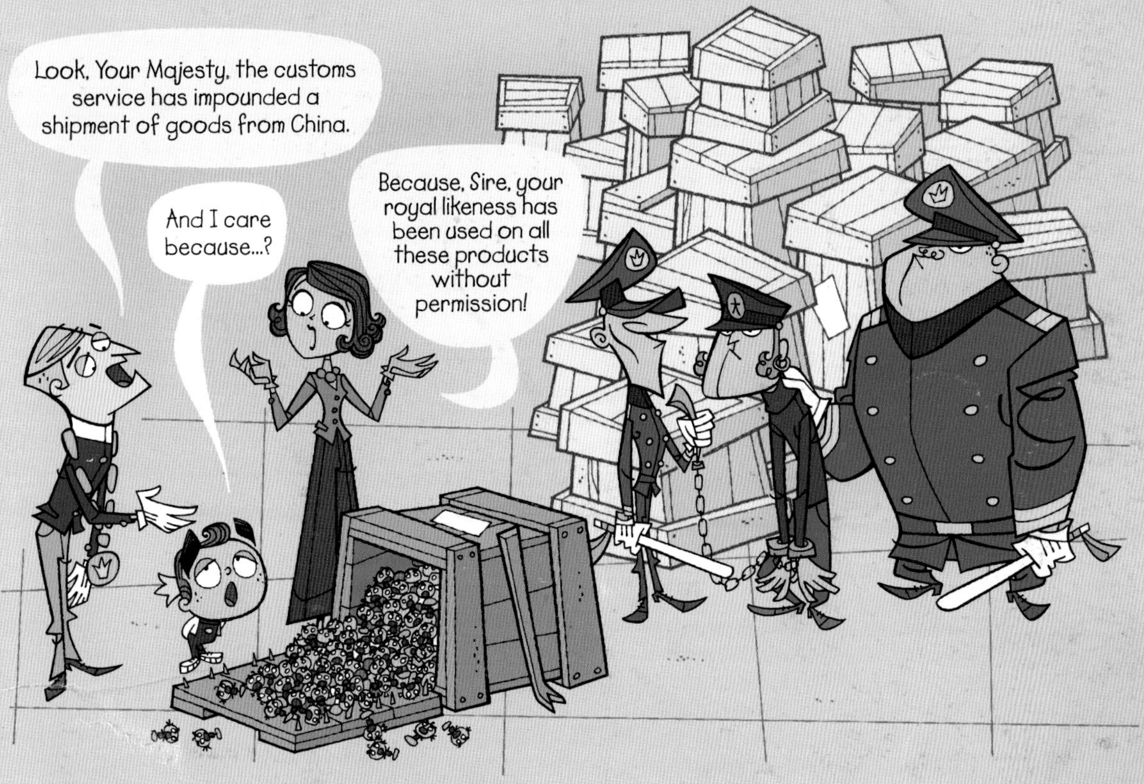
Look, Your Majesty, the customs service has impounded a shipment of goods from China.
And I care because...?
Because, Sire, your royal likeness has been used on all these products without permission!

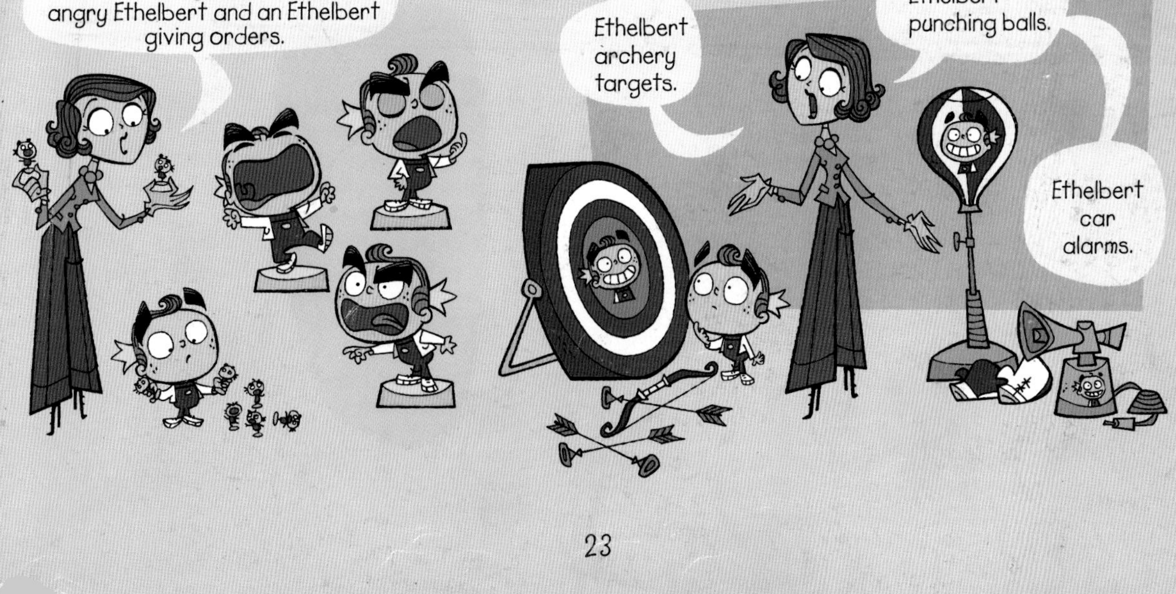
Plastic figurines of an angry Ethelbert and an Ethelbert giving orders.
Ethelbert archery targets.
Ethelbert punching balls.
Ethelbert car alarms.

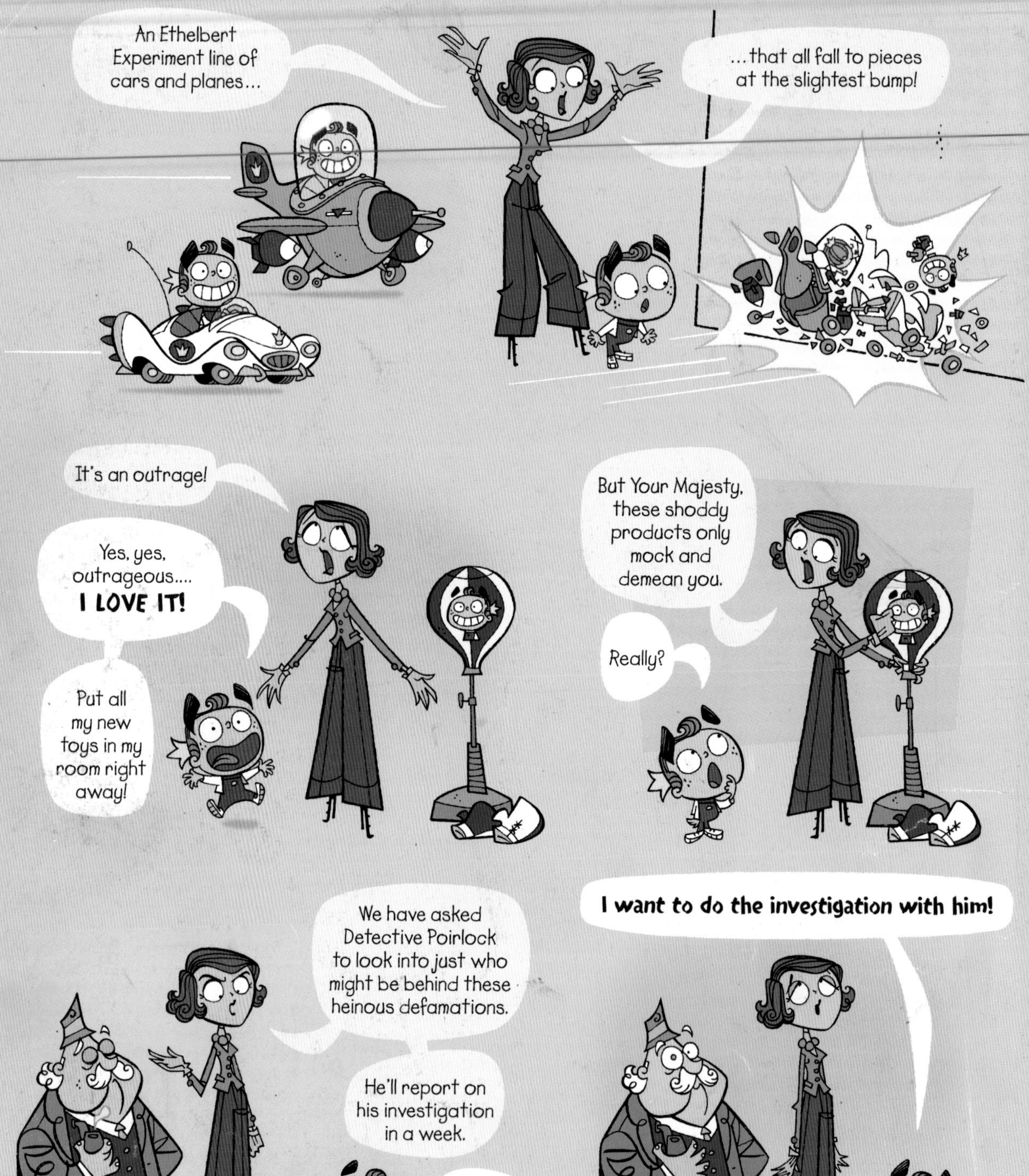
An Ethelbert Experiment line of cars and planes...
...that all fall to pieces at the slightest bump!
It's an outrage!
Yes, yes, outrageous....
I LOVE IT!
Put all my new toys in my room right away!
But Your Majesty, these shoddy products only mock and demean you.
Really?
We have asked Detective Poirlock to look into just who might be behind these heinous defamations.
He'll report on his investigation in a week.
Investigation?
I want to do the investigation with him!

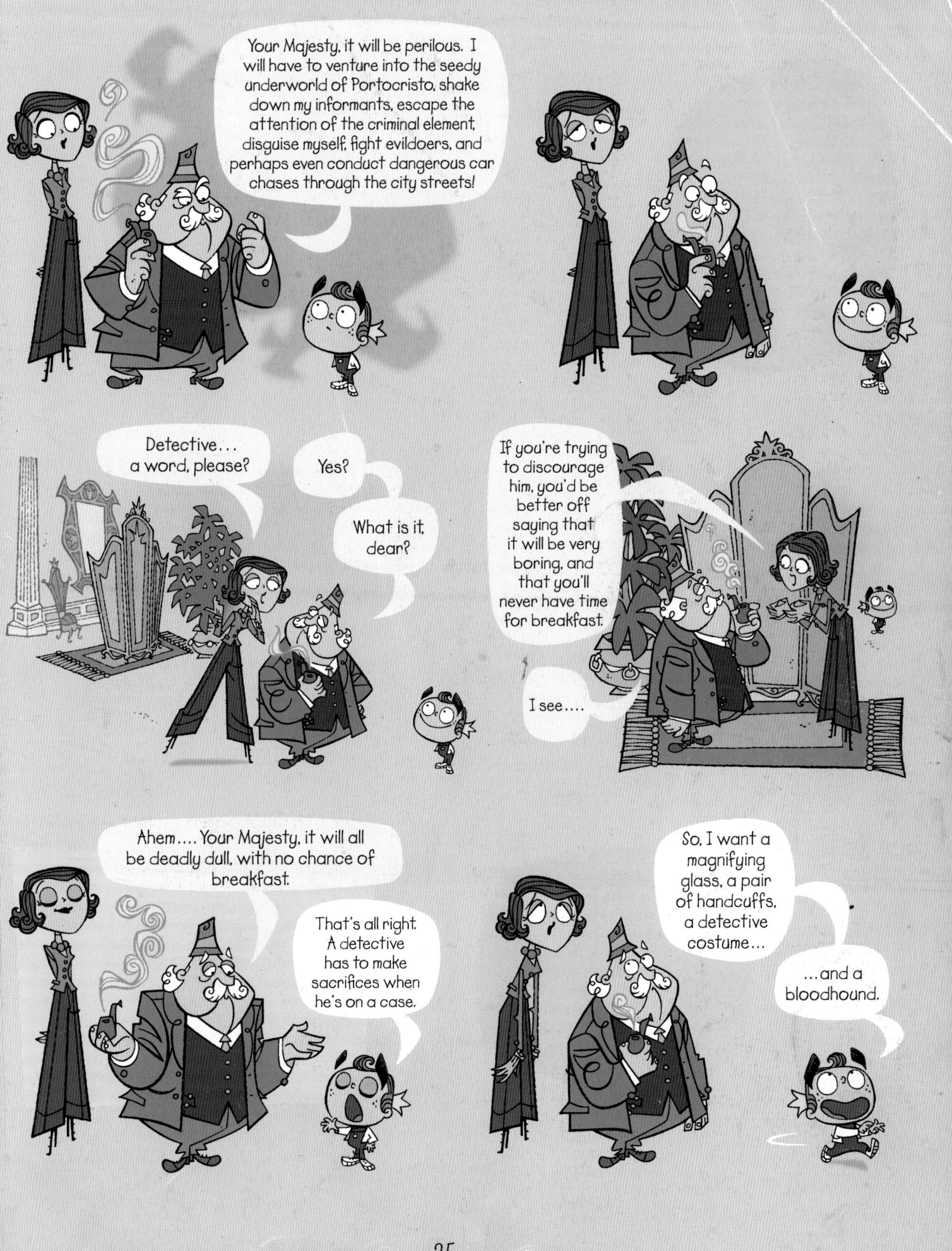
Your Majesty, it will be perilous. I will have to venture into the seedy underworld of Portocristo, shake down my informants, escape the attention of the criminal element, disguise myself, fight evildoers, and perhaps even conduct dangerous car chases through the city streets!
Detective... a word, please?
Yes?
What is it, dear?
If you're trying to discourage him, you'd be better off saying that it will be very boring, and that you'll never have time for breakfast.
I see....
Ahem.... Your Majesty, it will all be deadly dull, with no chance of breakfast.
That's all right. A detective has to make sacrifices when he's on a case.
So, I want a magnifying glass, a pair of handcuffs, a detective costume...
...and a bloodhound.

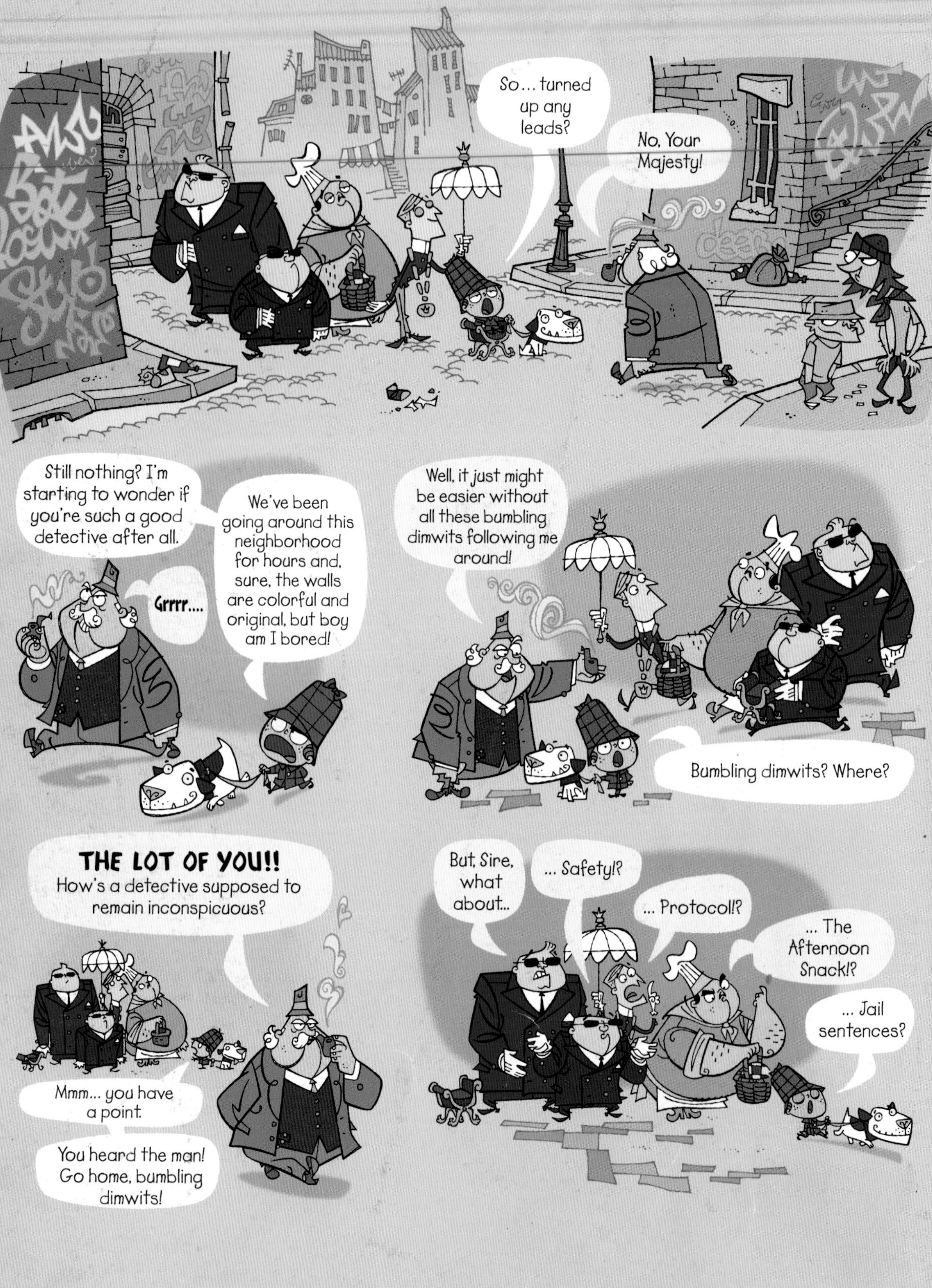

So... turned up any leads?
No, Your Majesty!
Still nothing? I'm starting to wonder if you're such a good detective after all.
Grrrr....
We've been going around this neighborhood for hours and, sure, the walls are colorful and original, but boy am I bored!
Well, it just might be easier without all these bumbling dimwits following me around!
Bumbling dimwits? Where?
THE LOT OF YOU!!
How's a detective supposed to remain inconspicuous?
Mmm... you have a point.
You heard the man! Go home, bumbling dimwits!
But, Sire, what about...
... Safety!?
... Protocol!?
... The Afternoon Snack!?
... Jail sentences?

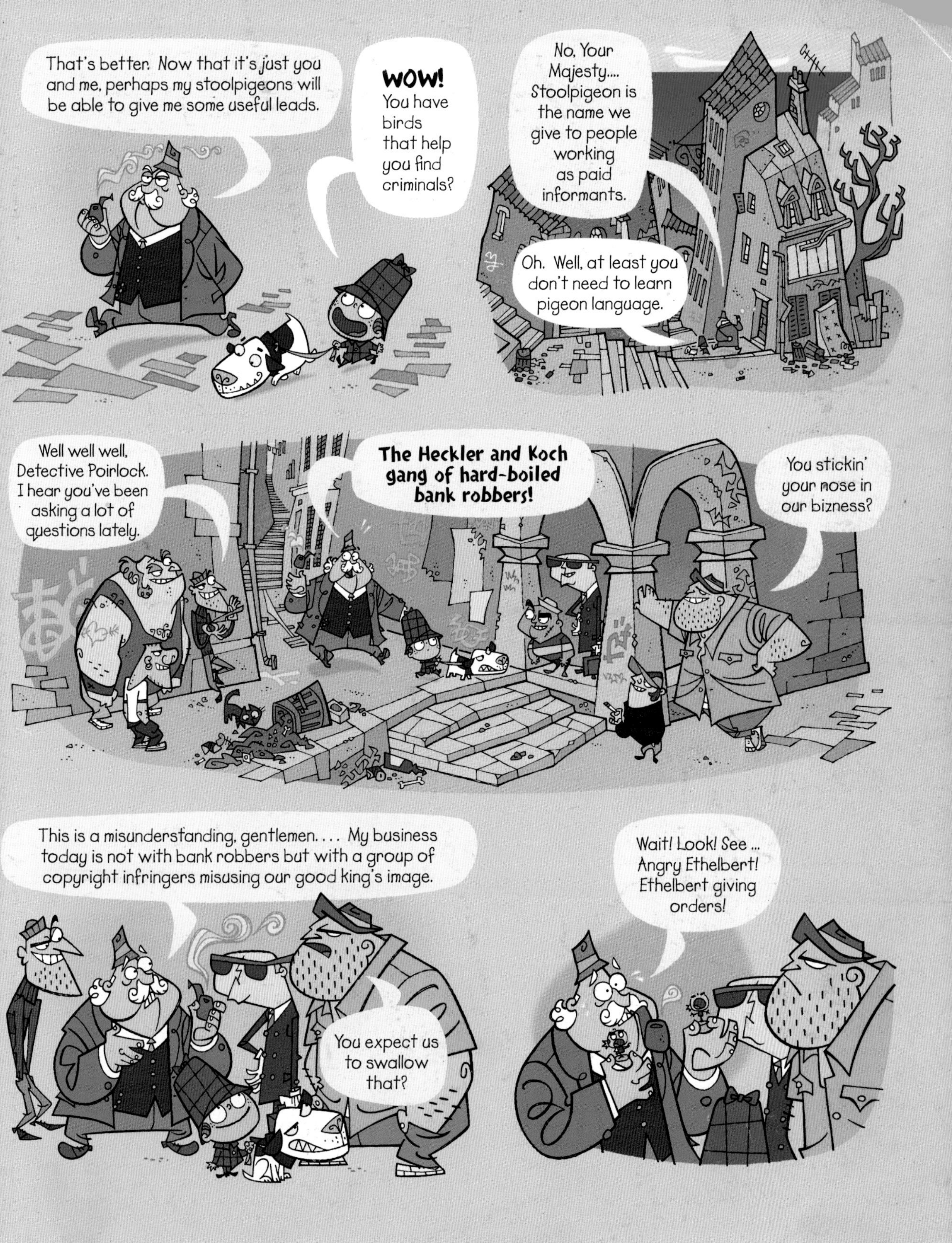
That's better. Now that it's just you and me, perhaps my stoolpigeons will be able to give me some useful leads.
WOW! You have birds that help you find criminals?
No, Your Majesty.... Stoolpigeon is the name we give to people working as paid informants.
Oh. Well, at least you don't need to learn pigeon language.
Well well well, Detective Poirlock. I hear you've been asking a lot of questions lately.
The Heckler and Koch gang of hard-boiled bank robbers!
You stickin' your nose in our bizness?
This is a misunderstanding, gentlemen.... My business today is not with bank robbers but with a group of copyright infringers misusing our good king's image.
You expect us to swallow that?
Wait! Look! See ... Angry Ethelbert! Ethelbert giving orders!

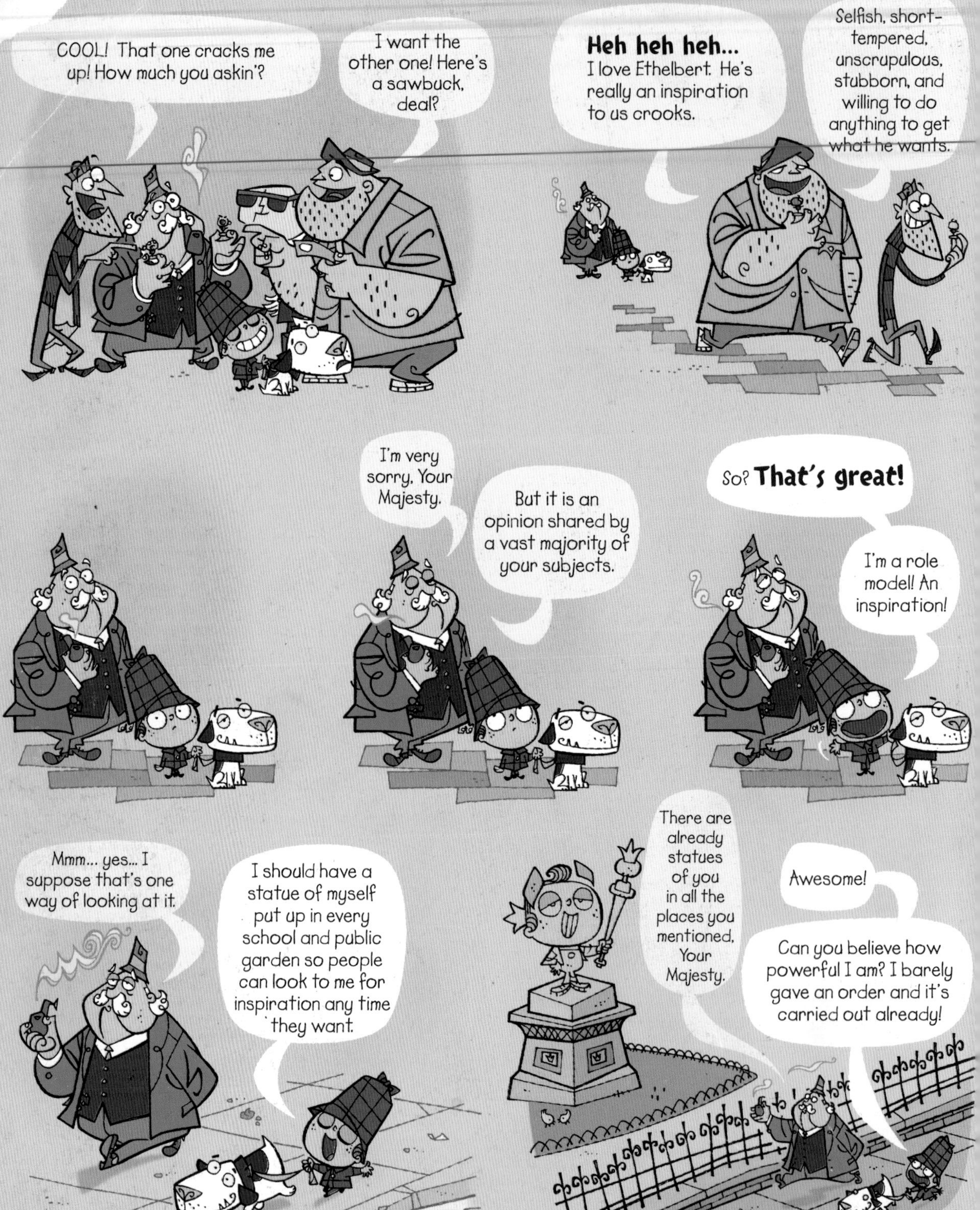
COOL! That one cracks me up! How much you askin'?
I want the other one! Here's a sawbuck, deal?
Heh heh heh... I love Ethelbert. He's really an inspiration to us crooks.
Selfish, short-tempered, unscrupulous, stubborn, and willing to do anything to get what he wants.
I'm very sorry, Your Majesty.
But it is an opinion shared by a vast majority of your subjects.
So? **That's great!**
I'm a role model! An inspiration!
Mmm... yes... I suppose that's one way of looking at it.
I should have a statue of myself put up in every school and public garden so people can look to me for inspiration any time they want.
There are already statues of you in all the places you mentioned, Your Majesty.
Awesome!
Can you believe how powerful I am? I barely gave an order and it's carried out already!

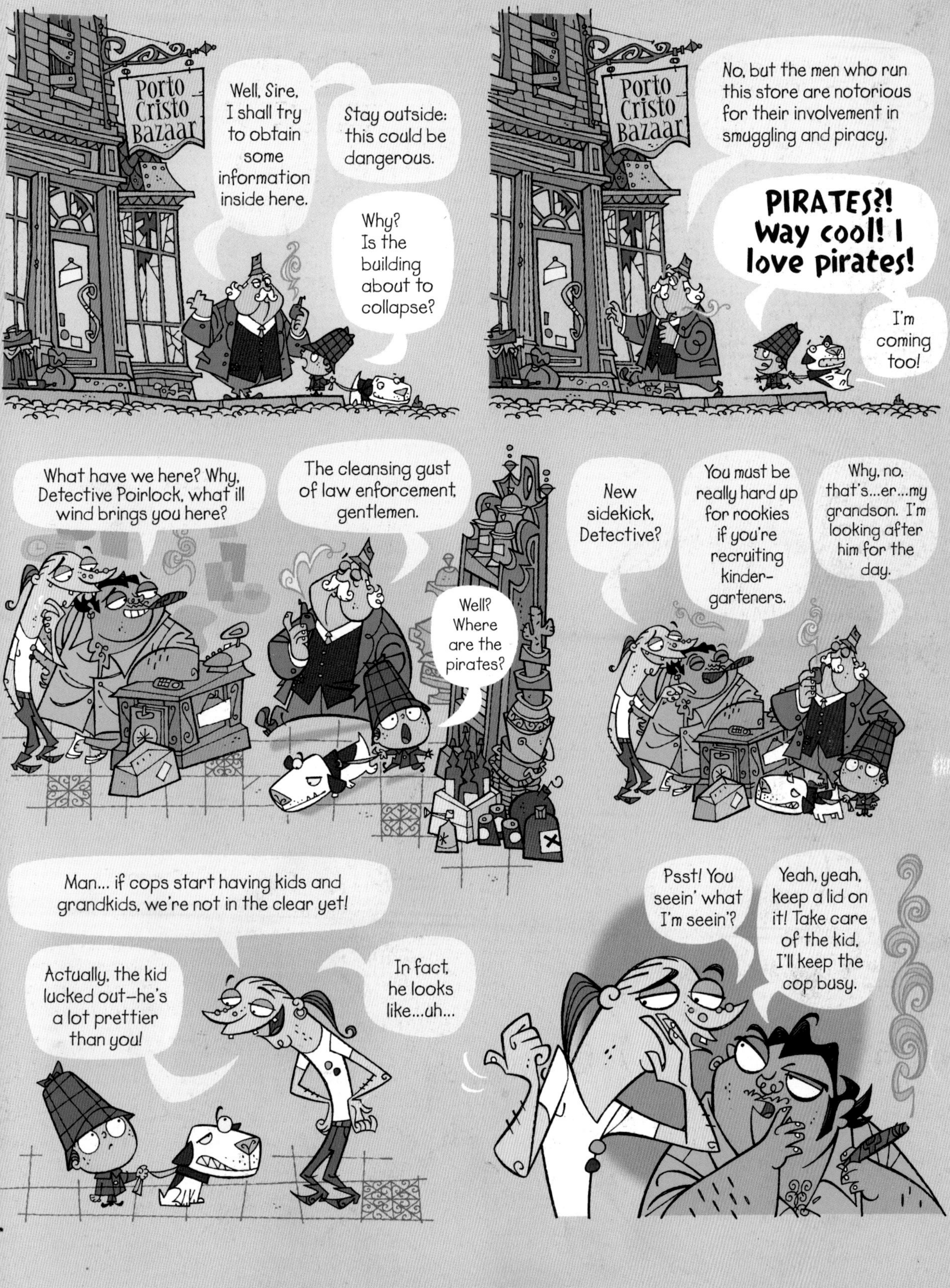
Porto Cristo Bazaar
Well, Sire, I shall try to obtain some information inside here.
Stay outside: this could be dangerous.
Why? Is the building about to collapse?
Porto Cristo Bazaar
No, but the men who run this store are notorious for their involvement in smuggling and piracy.
PIRATES?! Way cool! I love pirates!
I'm coming too!
What have we here? Why, Detective Poirlock, what ill wind brings you here?
The cleansing gust of law enforcement, gentlemen.
Well? Where are the pirates?
New sidekick, Detective?
You must be really hard up for rookies if you're recruiting kinder-garteners.
Why, no, that's...er...my grandson. I'm looking after him for the day.
Man... if cops start having kids and grandkids, we're not in the clear yet!
Actually, the kid lucked out—he's a lot prettier than you!
In fact, he looks like...uh...
Psst! You seein' what I'm seein'?
Yeah, yeah, keep a lid on it! Take care of the kid, I'll keep the cop busy.

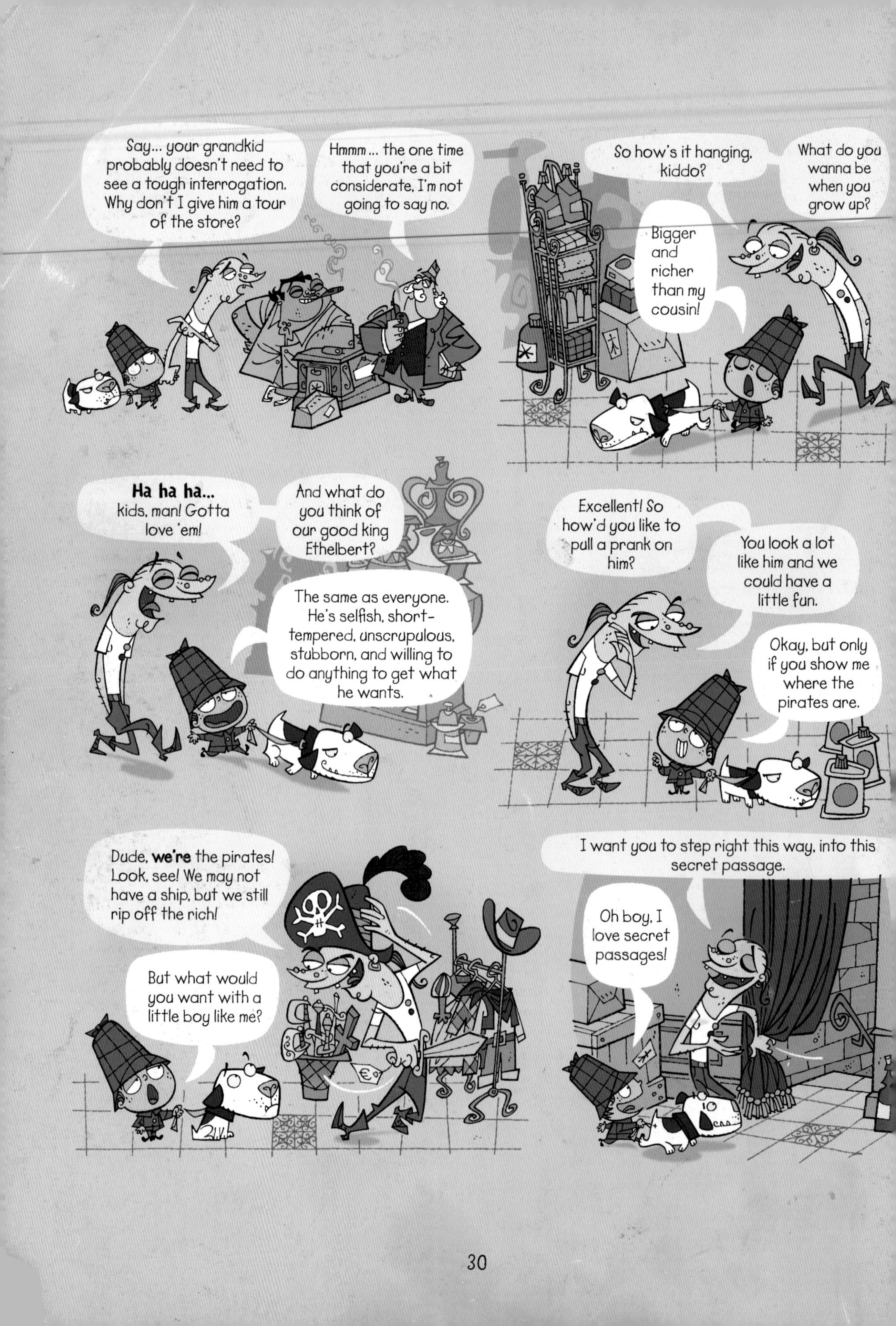
Say... your grandkid probably doesn't need to see a tough interrogation. Why don't I give him a tour of the store?
Hmmm... the one time that you're a bit considerate, I'm not going to say no.
So how's it hanging, kiddo?
What do you wanna be when you grow up?
Bigger and richer than my cousin!
Ha ha ha... kids, man! Gotta love 'em!
And what do you think of our good king Ethelbert?
The same as everyone. He's selfish, short-tempered, unscrupulous, stubborn, and willing to do anything to get what he wants.
Excellent! So how'd you like to pull a prank on him?
You look a lot like him and we could have a little fun.
Okay, but only if you show me where the pirates are.
Dude, **we're** the pirates! Look, see! We may not have a ship, but we still rip off the rich!
But what would you want with a little boy like me?
I want you to step right this way, into this secret passage.
Oh boy, I love secret passages!

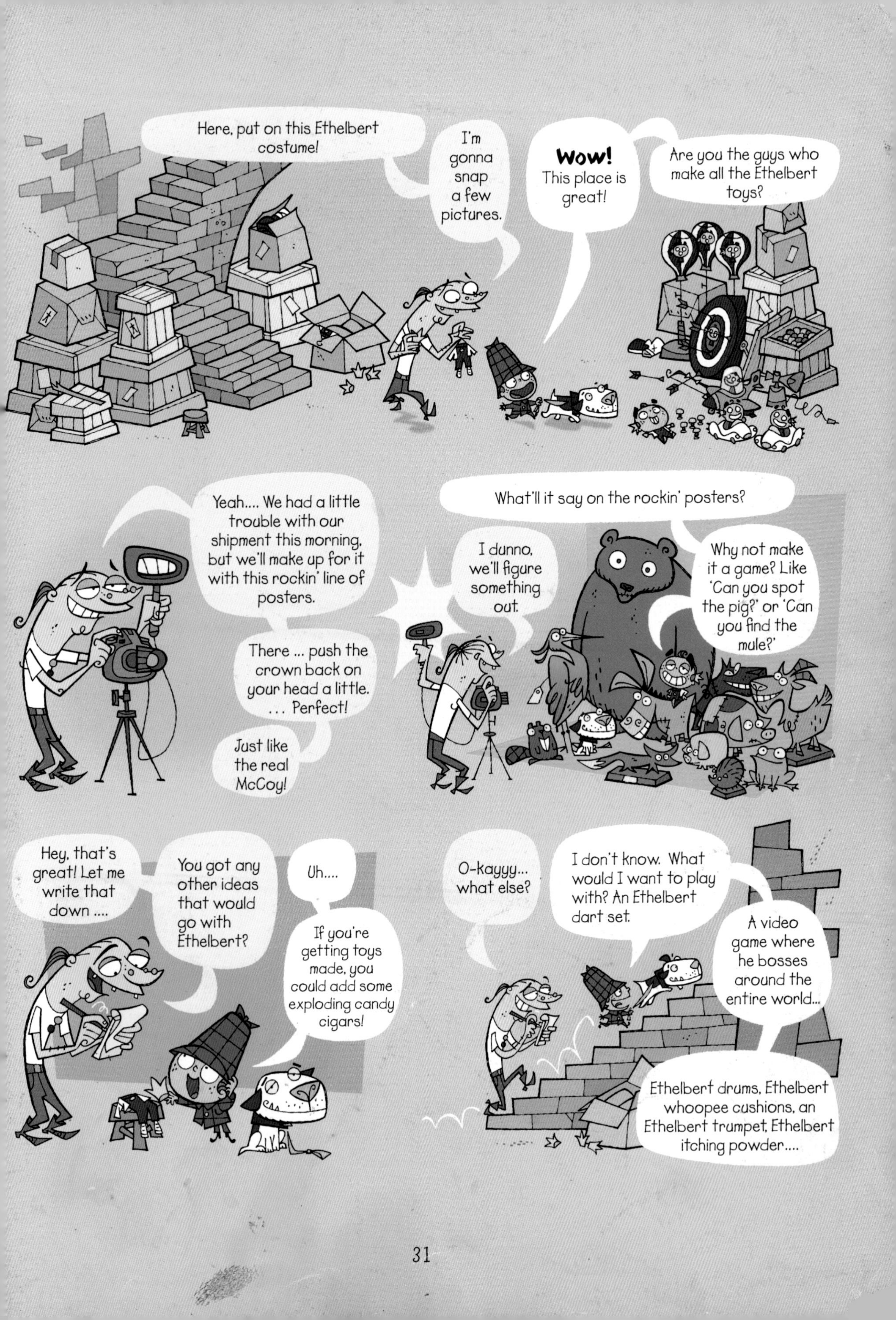
Here, put on this Ethelbert costume!
I'm gonna snap a few pictures.
Wow! This place is great!
Are you the guys who make all the Ethelbert toys?
Yeah.... We had a little trouble with our shipment this morning, but we'll make up for it with this rockin' line of posters.
There ... push the crown back on your head a little. ... Perfect!
Just like the real McCoy!
What'll it say on the rockin' posters?
I dunno, we'll figure something out.
Why not make it a game? Like 'Can you spot the pig?' or 'Can you find the mule?'
Hey, that's great! Let me write that down ....
You got any other ideas that would go with Ethelbert?
Uh....
If you're getting toys made, you could add some exploding candy cigars!
O-kayyy... what else?
I don't know. What would I want to play with? An Ethelbert dart set.
A video game where he bosses around the entire world...
Ethelbert drums, Ethelbert whoopee cushions, an Ethelbert trumpet, Ethelbert itching powder....

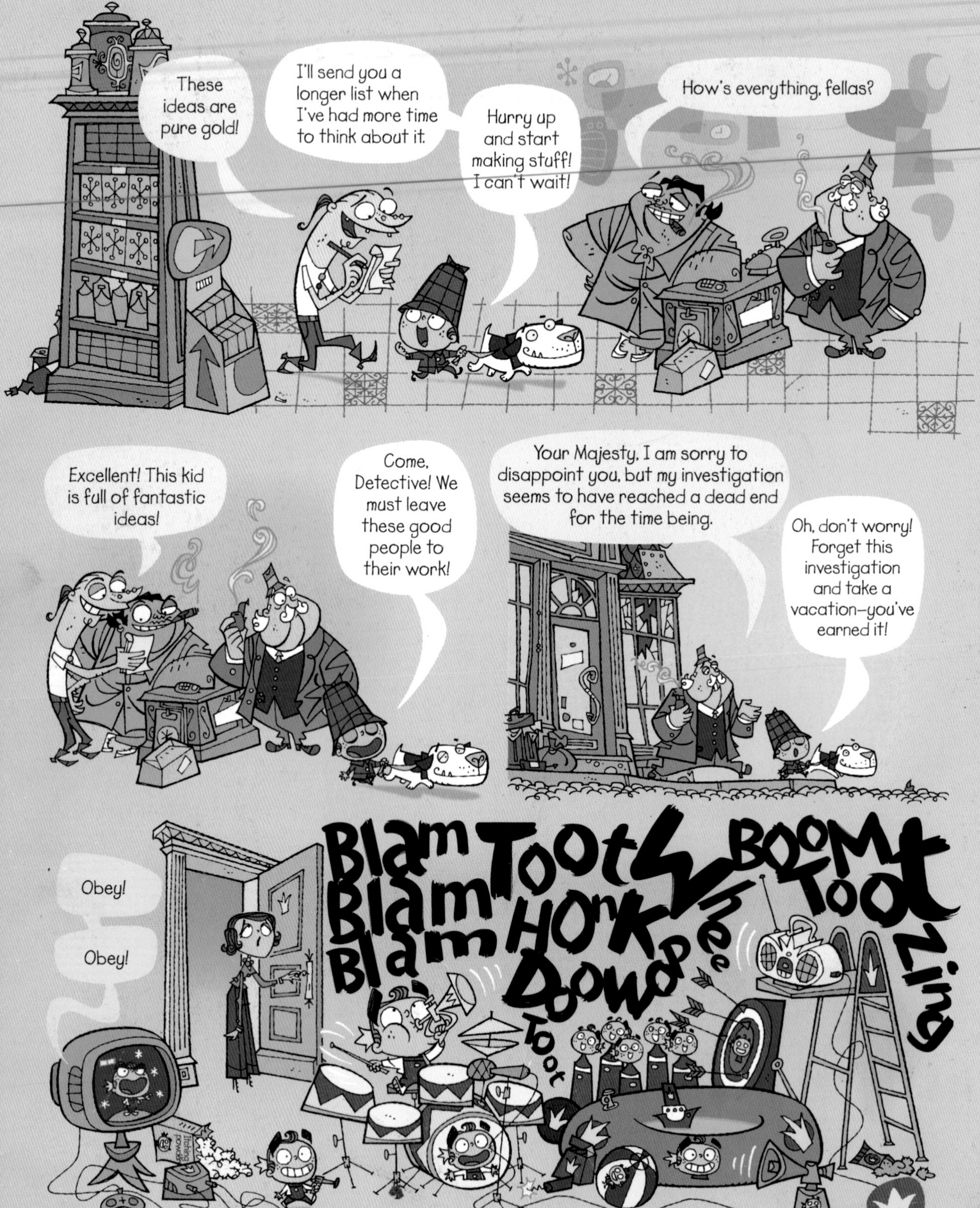
These ideas are pure gold!
I'll send you a longer list when I've had more time to think about it.
Hurry up and start making stuff! I can't wait!
How's everything, fellas?
Excellent! This kid is full of fantastic ideas!
Come, Detective! We must leave these good people to their work!
Your Majesty, I am sorry to disappoint you, but my investigation seems to have reached a dead end for the time being.
Oh, don't worry! Forget this investigation and take a vacation—you've earned it!
Obey!
Obey!
Blam
Blam
Blam
Toot
Honk
Doowop
Toot
Whee
BOOM
Toot
Zing
Itching powder

A Mountaintop Inheritance

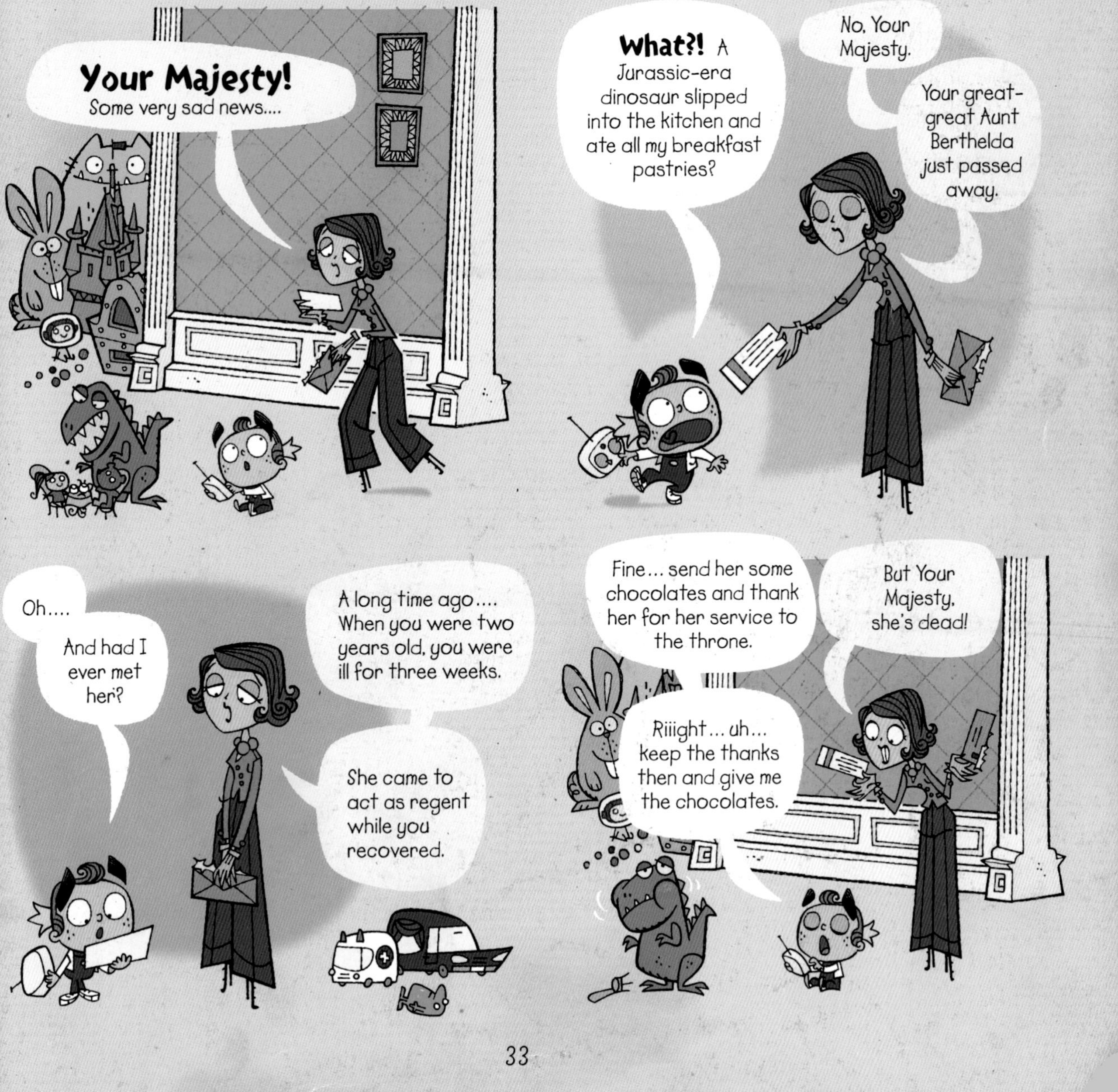

Your Majesty! Some very sad news....
What?! A Jurassic-era dinosaur slipped into the kitchen and ate all my breakfast pastries?
No, Your Majesty.
Your great-great Aunt Berthelda just passed away.
Oh....
And had I ever met her?
A long time ago.... When you were two years old, you were ill for three weeks.
She came to act as regent while you recovered.
Fine... send her some chocolates and thank her for her service to the throne.
But Your Majesty, she's dead!
Riiight... uh... keep the thanks then and give me the chocolates.

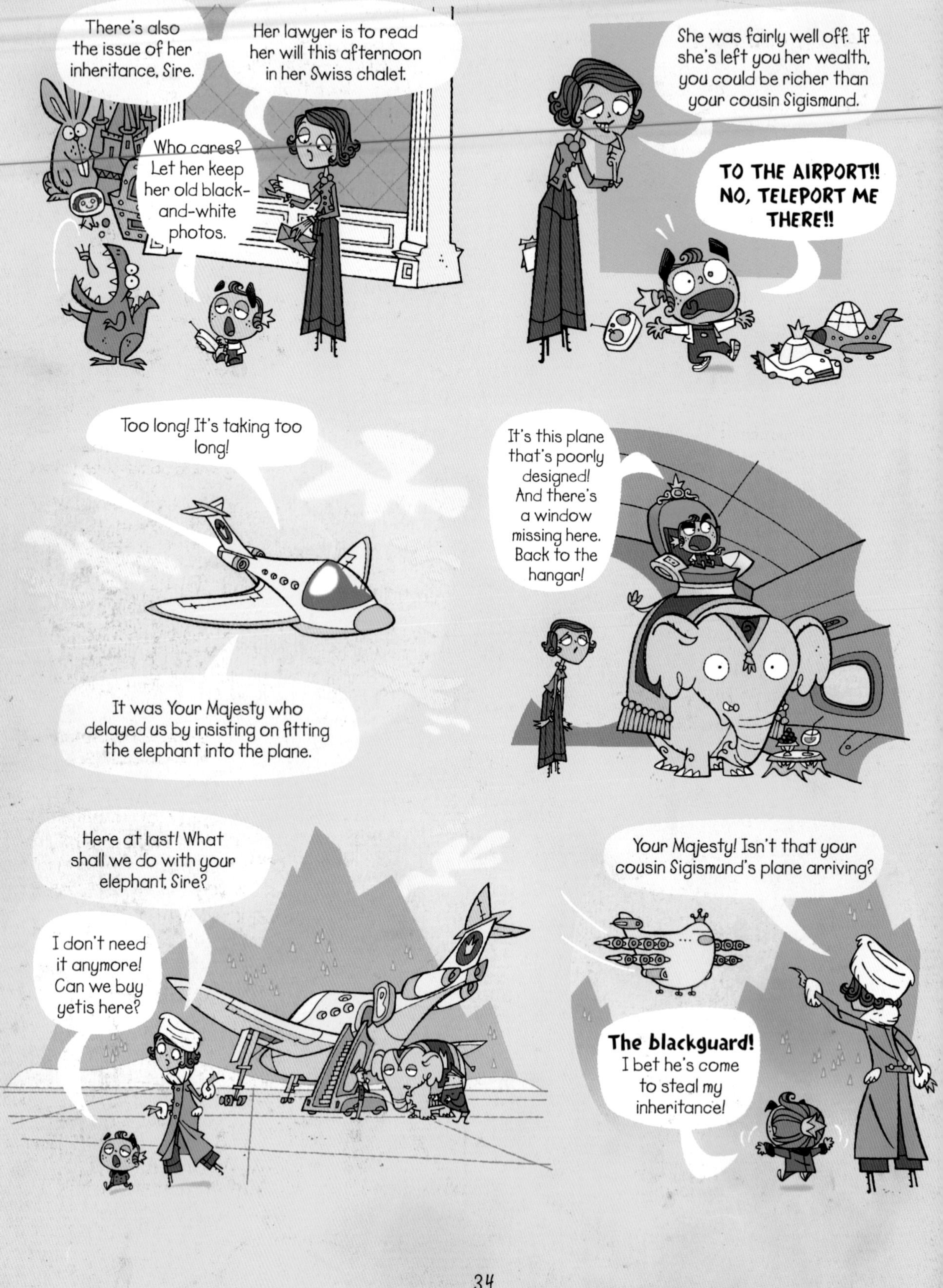

There's also the issue of her inheritance, Sire.
Her lawyer is to read her will this afternoon in her Swiss chalet.
Who cares? Let her keep her old black-and-white photos.
She was fairly well off. If she's left you her wealth, you could be richer than your cousin Sigismund.
TO THE AIRPORT!! NO, TELEPORT ME THERE!!
Too long! It's taking too long!
It was Your Majesty who delayed us by insisting on fitting the elephant into the plane.
It's this plane that's poorly designed! And there's a window missing here. Back to the hangar!
Here at last! What shall we do with your elephant, Sire?
I don't need it anymore! Can we buy yetis here?
Your Majesty! Isn't that your cousin Sigismund's plane arriving?
The blackguard! I bet he's come to steal my inheritance!

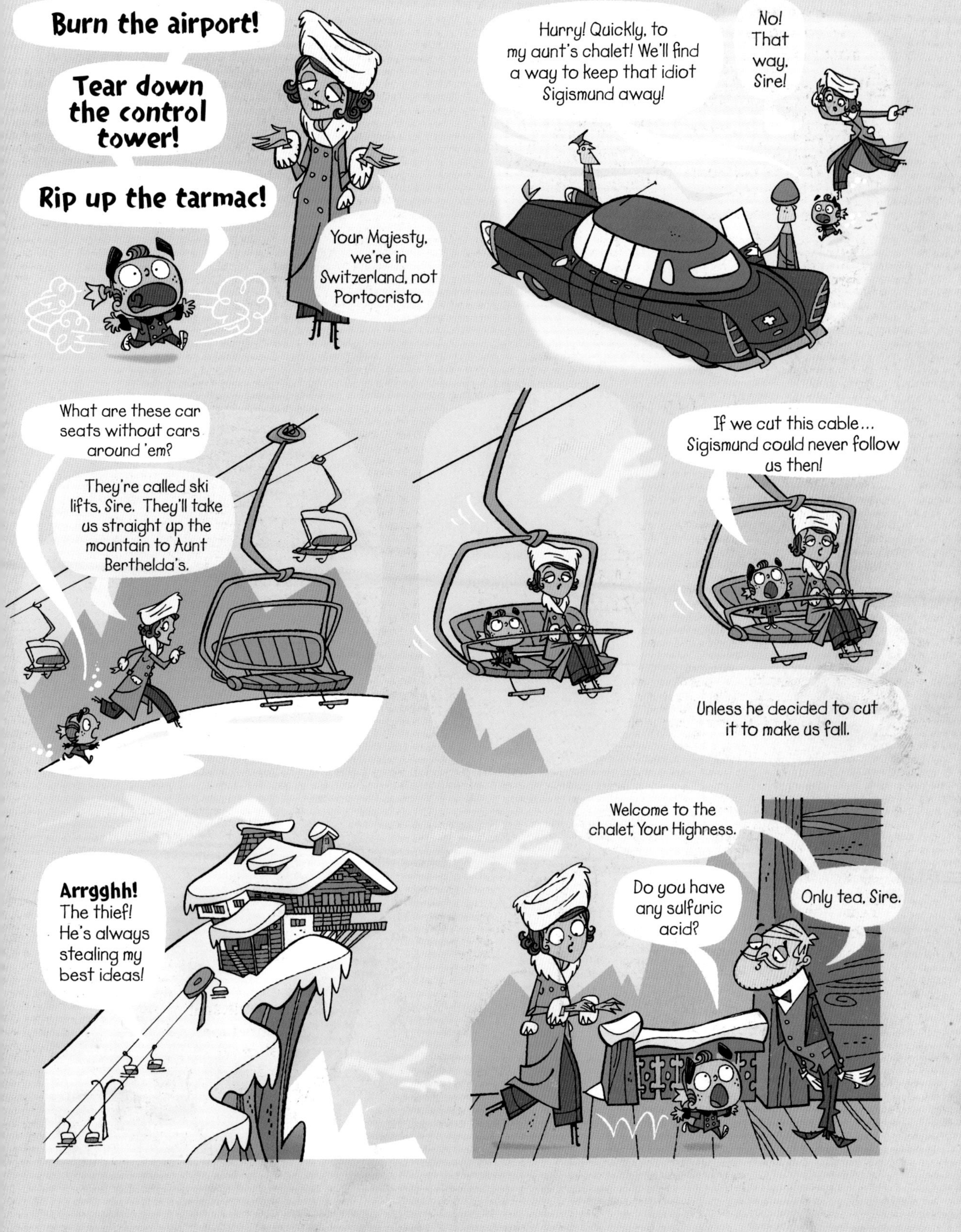
Burn the airport!
Tear down the control tower!
Rip up the tarmac!
Your Majesty, we're in Switzerland, not Portocristo.
Hurry! Quickly, to my aunt's chalet! We'll find a way to keep that idiot Sigismund away!
No! That way, Sire!
What are these car seats without cars around 'em?
They're called ski lifts, Sire. They'll take us straight up the mountain to Aunt Berthelda's.
If we cut this cable... Sigismund could never follow us then!
Unless he decided to cut it to make us fall.
Arrgghh! The thief! He's always stealing my best ideas!
Welcome to the chalet, Your Highness.
Do you have any sulfuric acid?
Only tea, Sire.

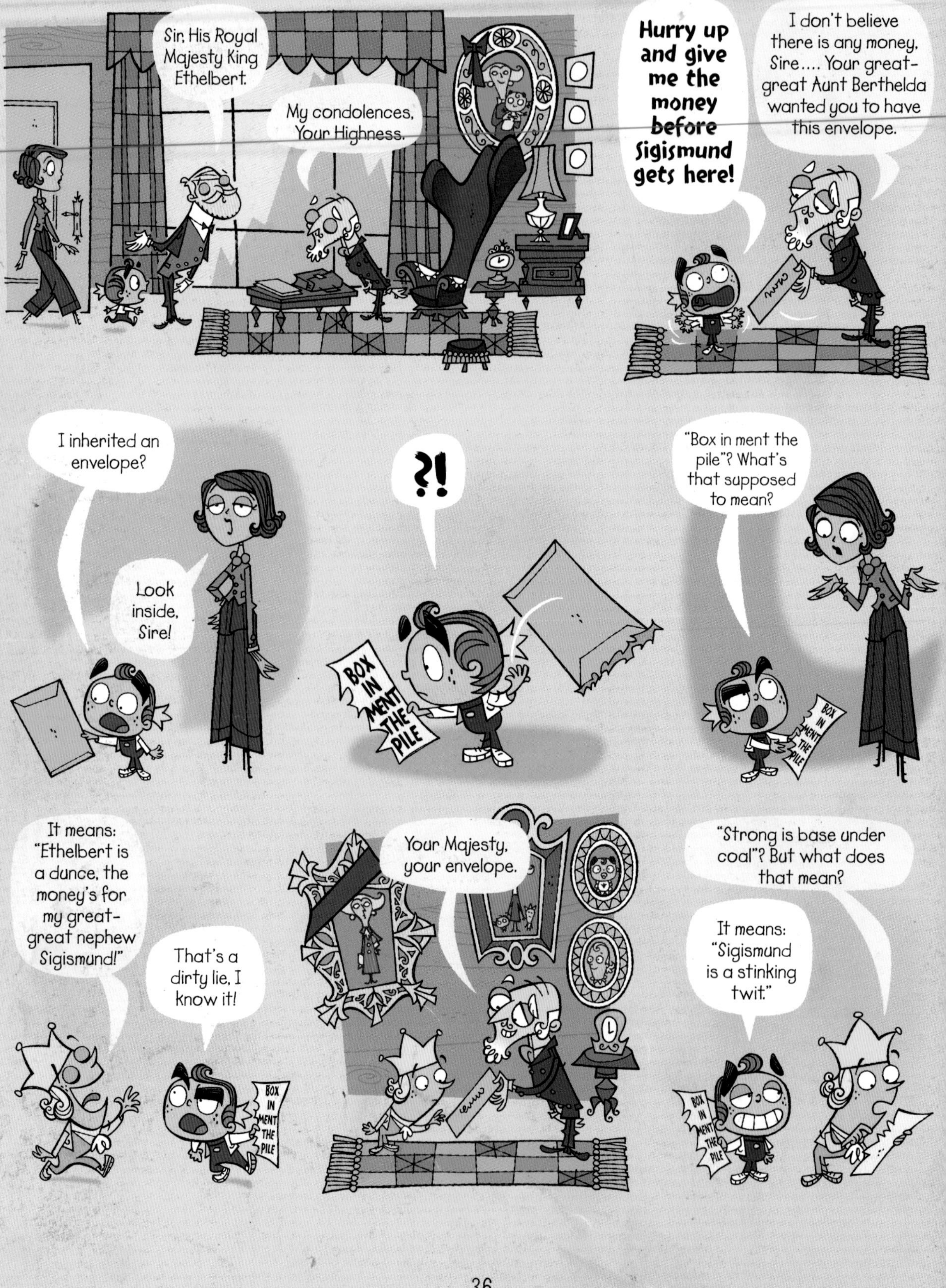

Sir, His Royal Majesty King Ethelbert.
My condolences, Your Highness.
Hurry up and give me the money before Sigismund gets here!
I don't believe there is any money, Sire.... Your great-great Aunt Berthelda wanted you to have this envelope.
I inherited an envelope?
Look inside, Sire!
?!
BOX IN MENT THE PILE
"Box in ment the pile"? What's that supposed to mean?
BOX IN MENT THE PILE
It means: "Ethelbert is a dunce, the money's for my great-great nephew Sigismund!"
That's a dirty lie, I know it!
BOX IN MENT THE PILE
Your Majesty, your envelope.
"Strong is base under coal"? But what does that mean?
It means: "Sigismund is a stinking twit."
BOX IN MENT THE PILE

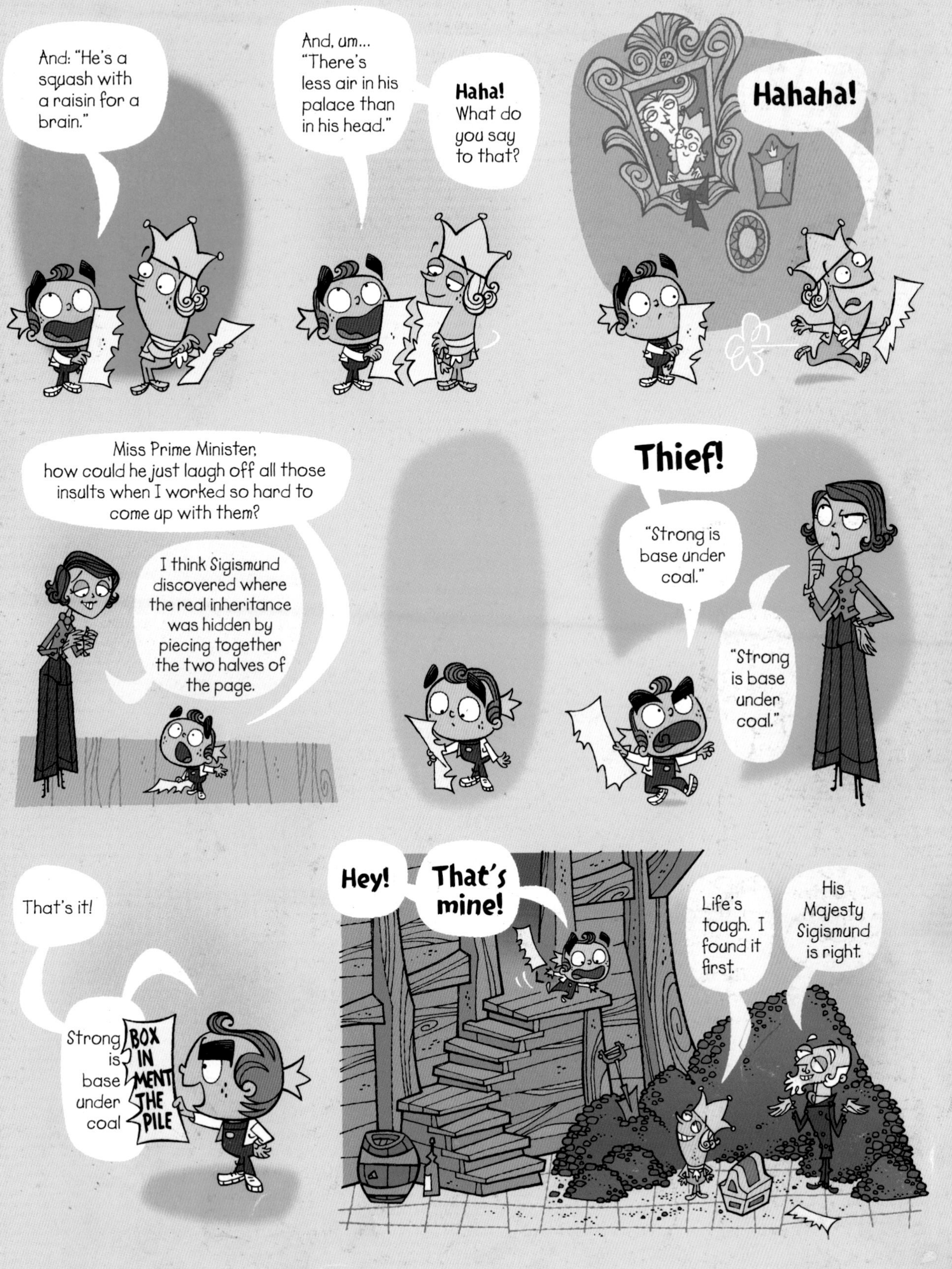

And: "He's a squash with a raisin for a brain."
And, um... "There's less air in his palace than in his head."
Haha! What do you say to that?
Hahaha!
Miss Prime Minister, how could he just laugh off all those insults when I worked so hard to come up with them?
I think Sigismund discovered where the real inheritance was hidden by piecing together the two halves of the page.
Thief!
"Strong is base under coal."
"Strong is base under coal."
That's it!
Strong is base under coal
BOX IN MENT THE PILE
Hey!
That's mine!
Life's tough. I found it first.
His Majesty Sigismund is right.

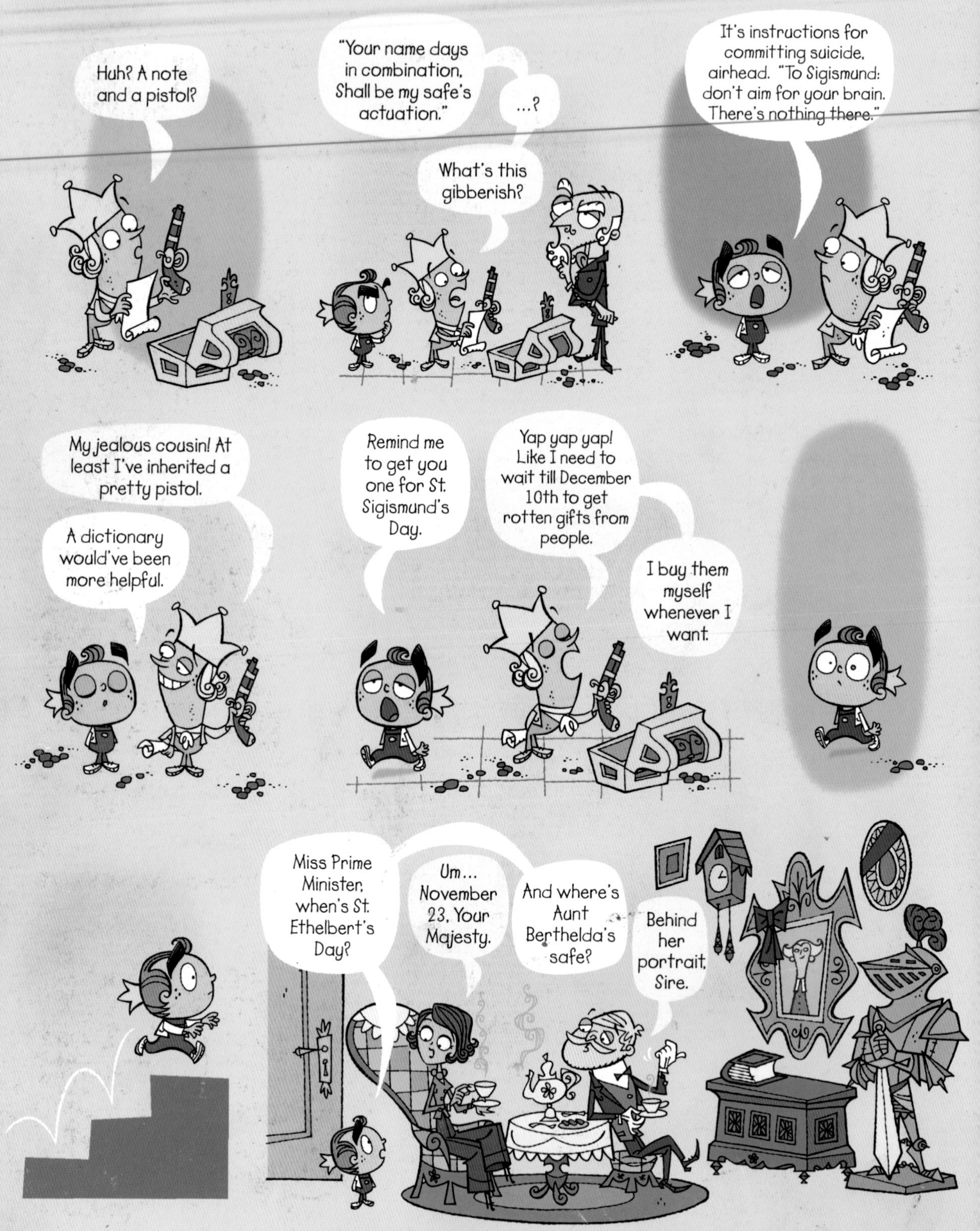
Huh? A note and a pistol?
"Your name days in combination, Shall be my safe's actuation."
...?
What's this gibberish?
It's instructions for committing suicide, airhead. "To Sigismund: don't aim for your brain. There's nothing there."
My jealous cousin! At least I've inherited a pretty pistol.
A dictionary would've been more helpful.
Remind me to get you one for St. Sigismund's Day.
Yap yap yap! Like I need to wait till December 10th to get rotten gifts from people.
I buy them myself whenever I want.
Miss Prime Minister, when's St. Ethelbert's Day?
Um... November 23, Your Majesty.
And where's Aunt Berthelda's safe?
Behind her portrait, Sire.

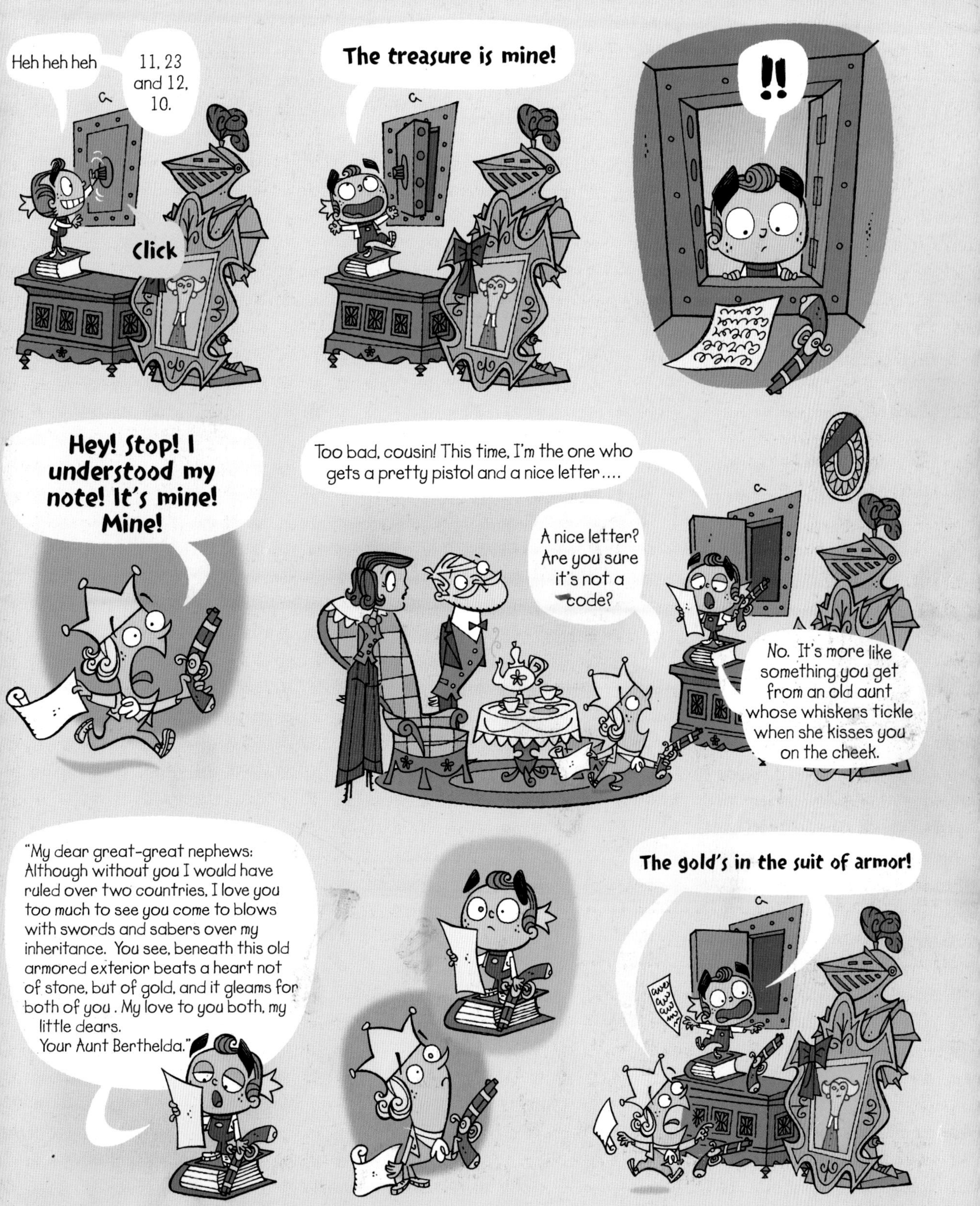

Heh heh heh
11, 23 and 12, 10.
Click
The treasure is mine!
!!
Hey! Stop! I understood my note! It's mine! Mine!
Too bad, cousin! This time, I'm the one who gets a pretty pistol and a nice letter....
A nice letter? Are you sure it's not a code?
No. It's more like something you get from an old aunt whose whiskers tickle when she kisses you on the cheek.
"My dear great-great nephews: Although without you I would have ruled over two countries, I love you too much to see you come to blows with swords and sabers over my inheritance. You see, beneath this old armored exterior beats a heart not of stone, but of gold, and it gleams for both of you. My love to you both, my little dears. Your Aunt Berthelda."
The gold's in the suit of armor!

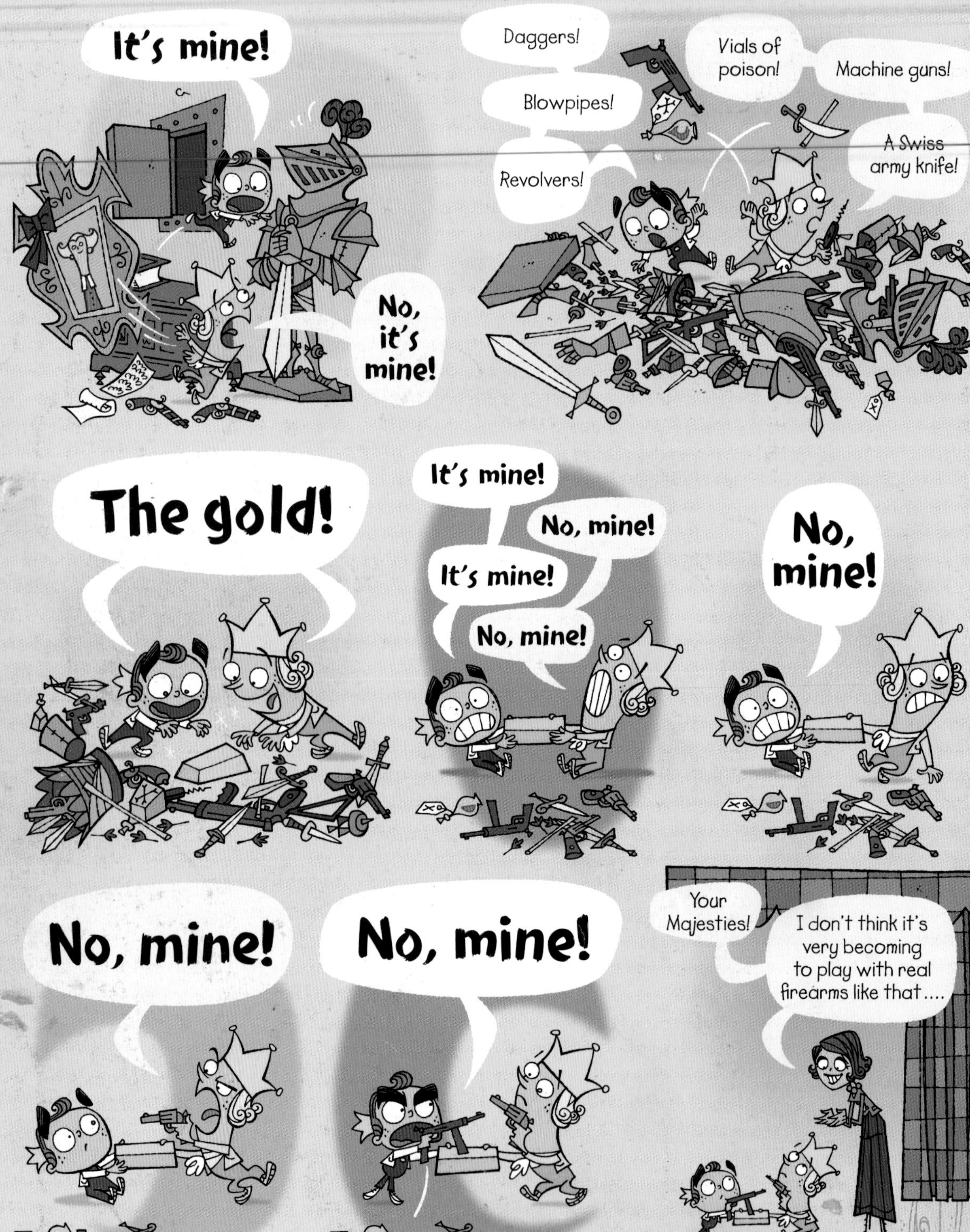
It's mine!
No, it's mine!
Daggers!
Blowpipes!
Revolvers!
Vials of poison!
Machine guns!
A Swiss army knife!
The gold!
It's mine!
No, mine!
It's mine!
No, mine!
No, mine!
No, mine!
No, mine!
Your Majesties!
I don't think it's very becoming to play with real firearms like that....

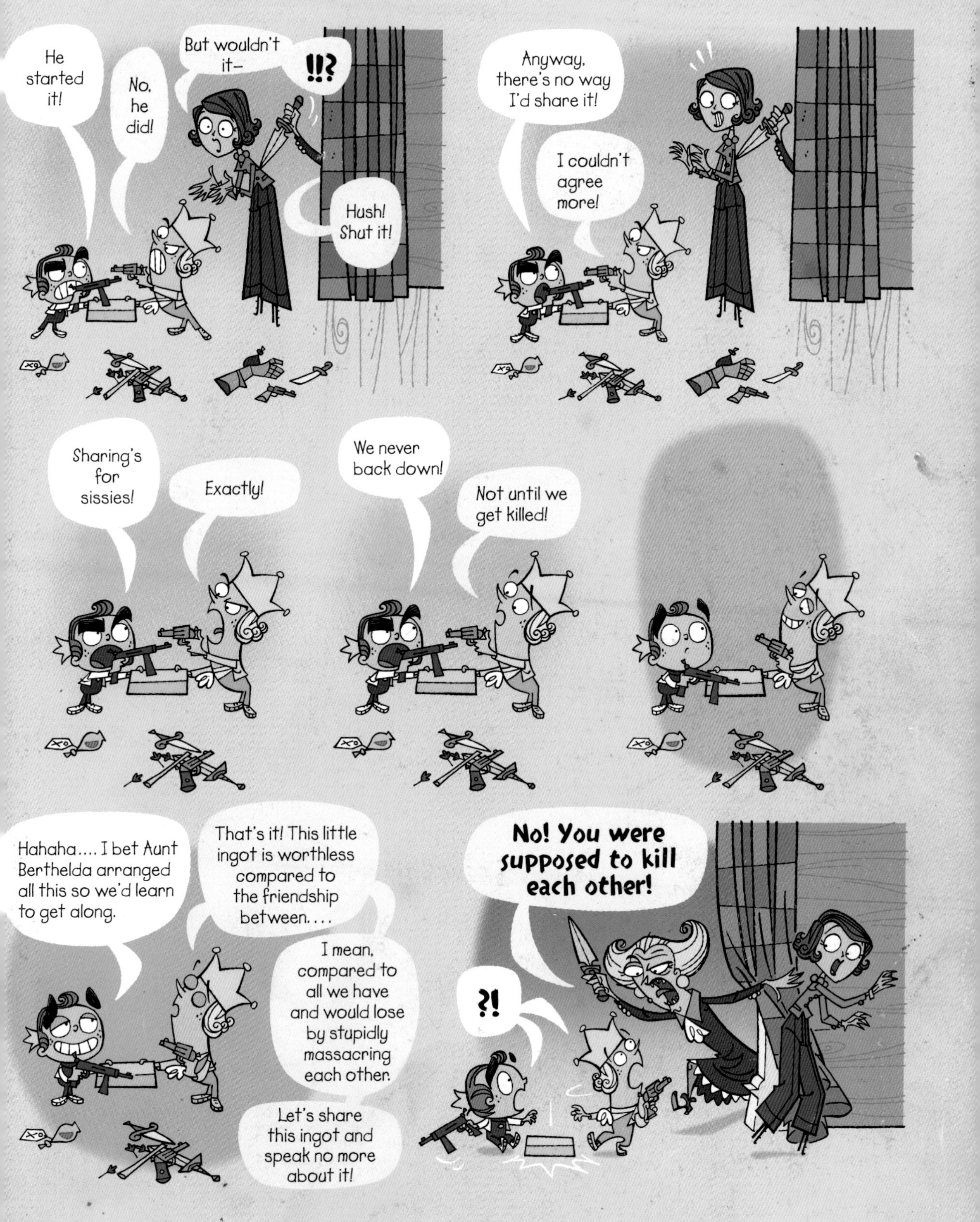
He started it!
No, he did!
But wouldn't it–
!!?
Hush! Shut it!
Anyway, there's no way I'd share it!
I couldn't agree more!
Sharing's for sissies!
Exactly!
We never back down!
Not until we get killed!
Hahaha.... I bet Aunt Berthelda arranged all this so we'd learn to get along.
That's it! This little ingot is worthless compared to the friendship between....
I mean, compared to all we have and would lose by stupidly massacring each other.
Let's share this ingot and speak no more about it!
No! You were supposed to kill each other!
?!

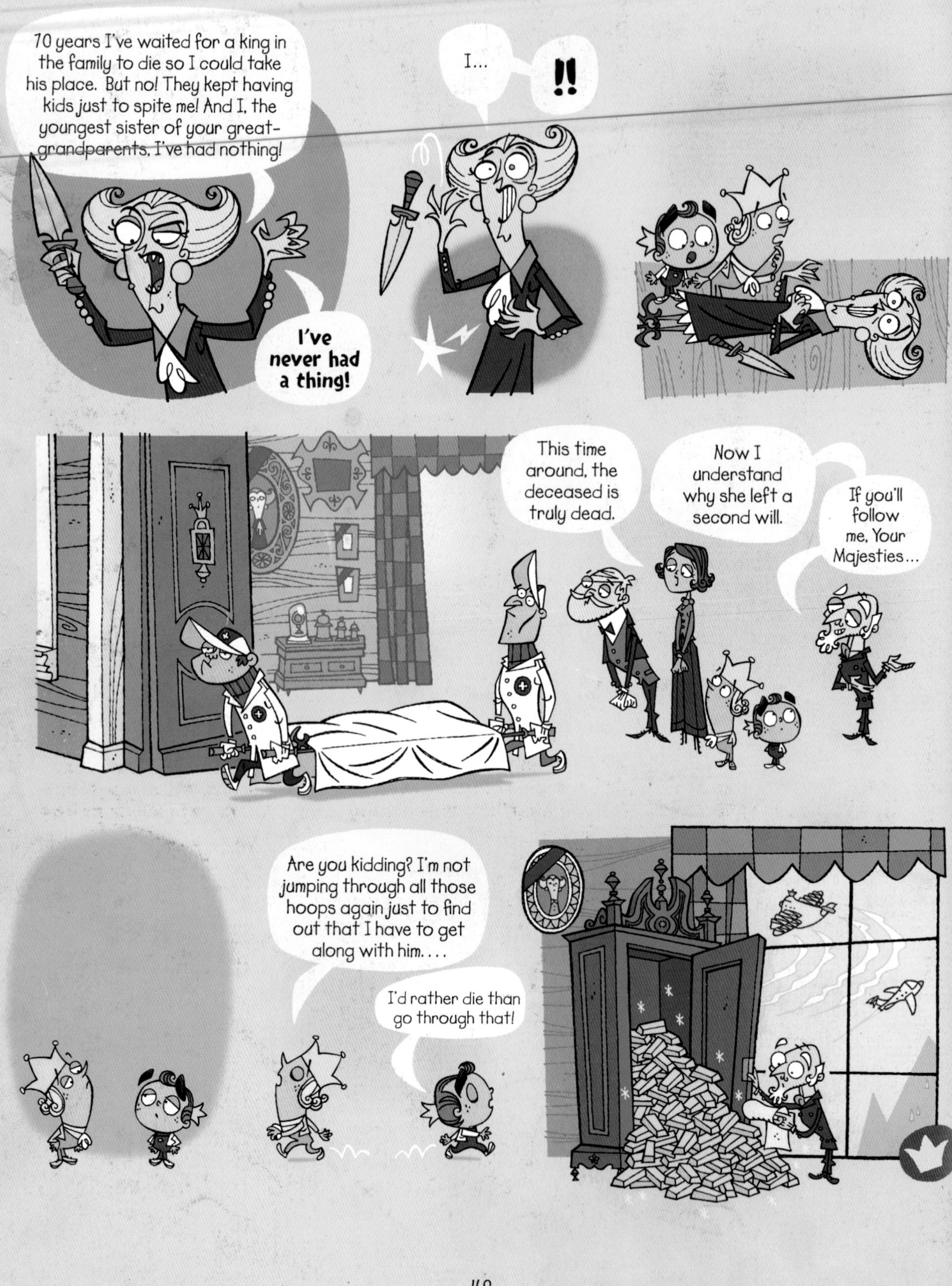

70 years I've waited for a king in the family to die so I could take his place. But no! They kept having kids just to spite me! And I, the youngest sister of your great-grandparents, I've had nothing!
I've never had a thing!
I...
!!
This time around, the deceased is truly dead.
Now I understand why she left a second will.
If you'll follow me, Your Majesties...
Are you kidding? I'm not jumping through all those hoops again just to find out that I have to get along with him. . . .
I'd rather die than go through that!

Rightsizing

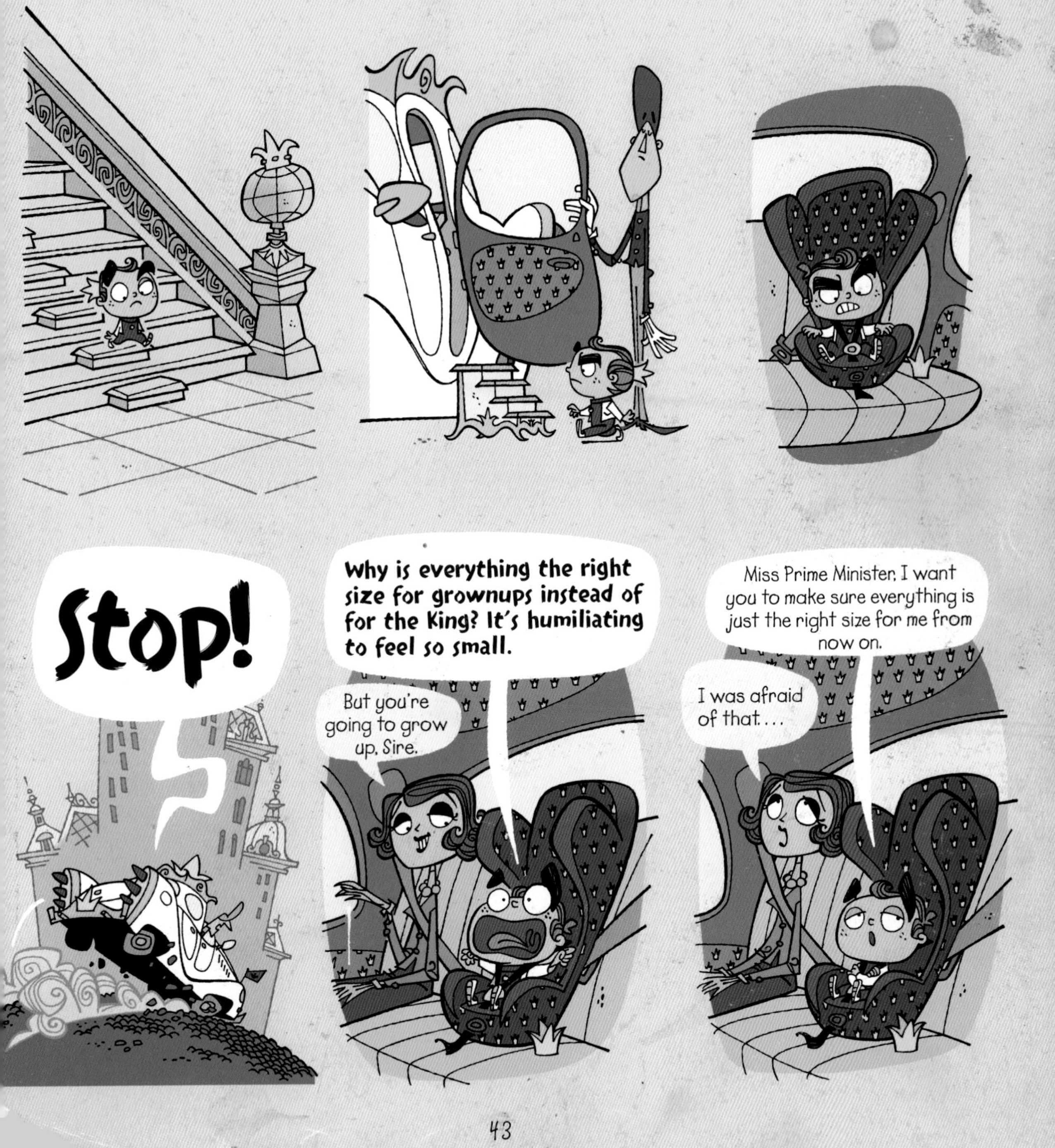
Stop!
Why is everything the right size for grownups instead of for the King? It's humiliating to feel so small.
But you're going to grow up, Sire.
Miss Prime Minister, I want you to make sure everything is just the right size for me from now on.
I was afraid of that. . . .

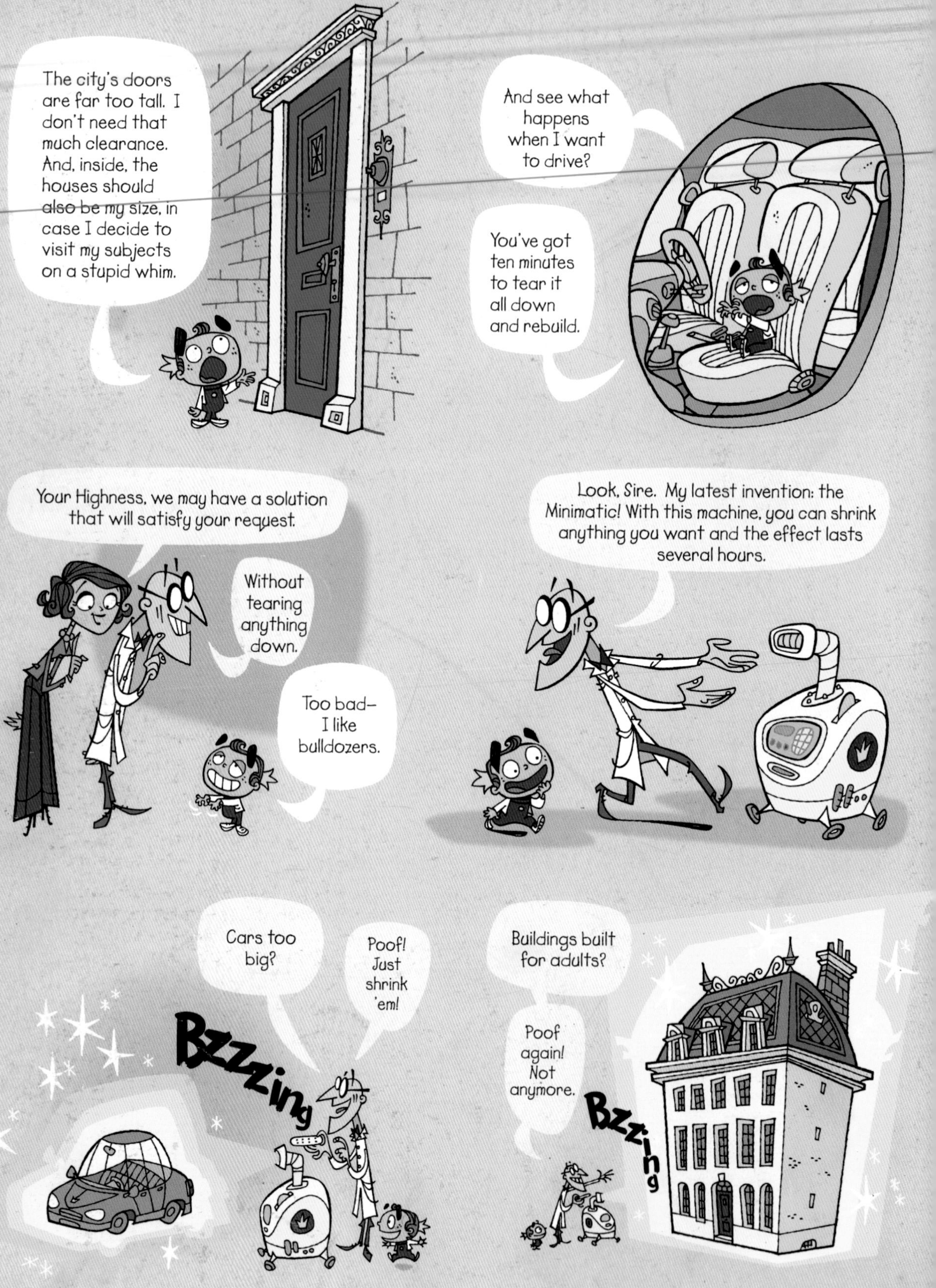

The city's doors are far too tall. I don't need that much clearance. And, inside, the houses should also be my size, in case I decide to visit my subjects on a stupid whim.
And see what happens when I want to drive?
You've got ten minutes to tear it all down and rebuild.
Your Highness, we may have a solution that will satisfy your request.
Without tearing anything down.
Too bad— I like bulldozers.
Look, Sire. My latest invention: the Minimatic! With this machine, you can shrink anything you want and the effect lasts several hours.
Cars too big?
Poof! Just shrink 'em!
Bzzzing
Buildings built for adults?
Poof again! Not anymore.
Bzzing

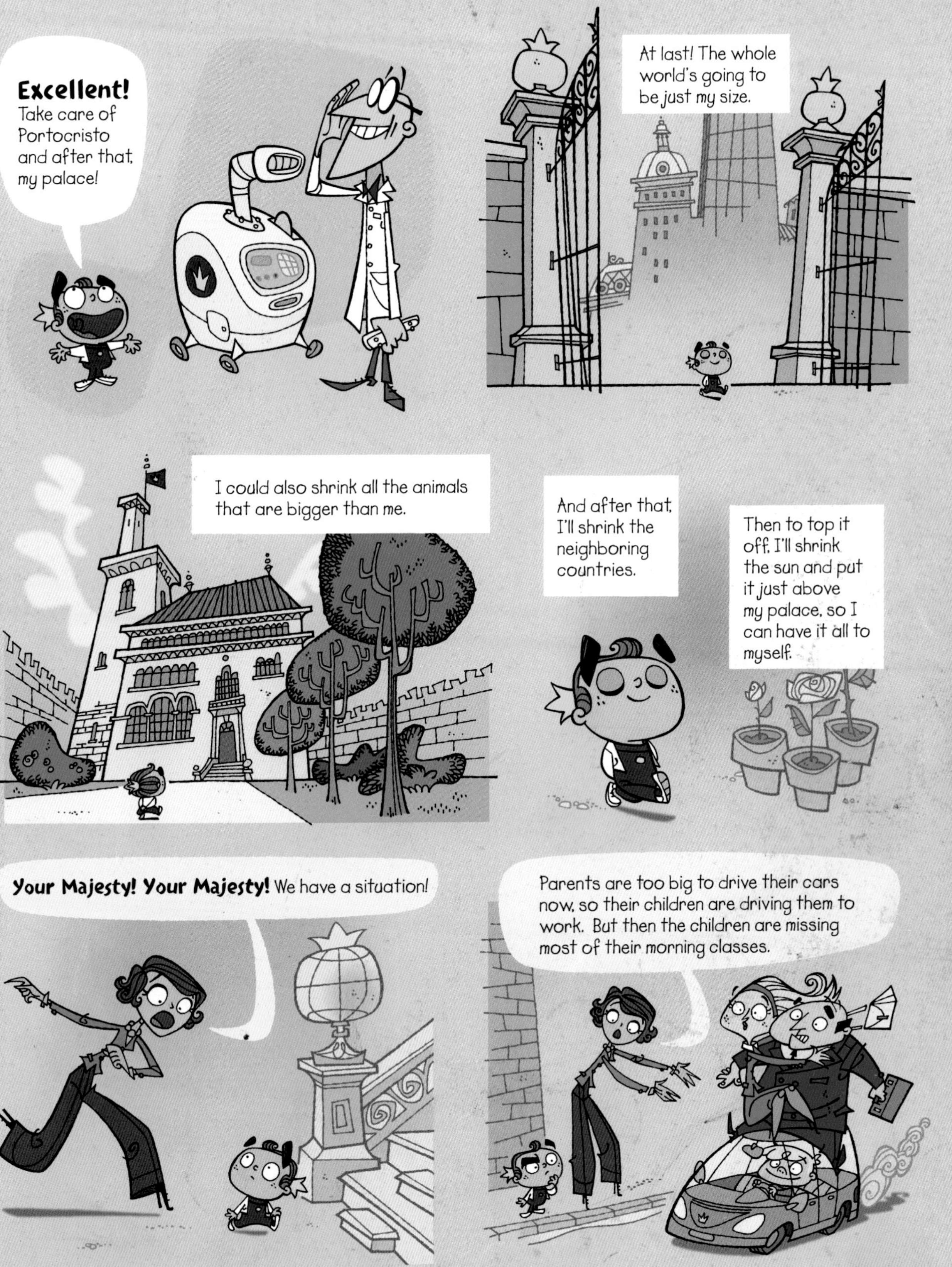
Excellent! Take care of Portocristo and after that, my palace!
At last! The whole world's going to be just my size.
I could also shrink all the animals that are bigger than me.
And after that, I'll shrink the neighboring countries.
Then to top it off, I'll shrink the sun and put it just above my palace, so I can have it all to myself.
Your Majesty! Your Majesty! We have a situation!
Parents are too big to drive their cars now, so their children are driving them to work. But then the children are missing most of their morning classes.

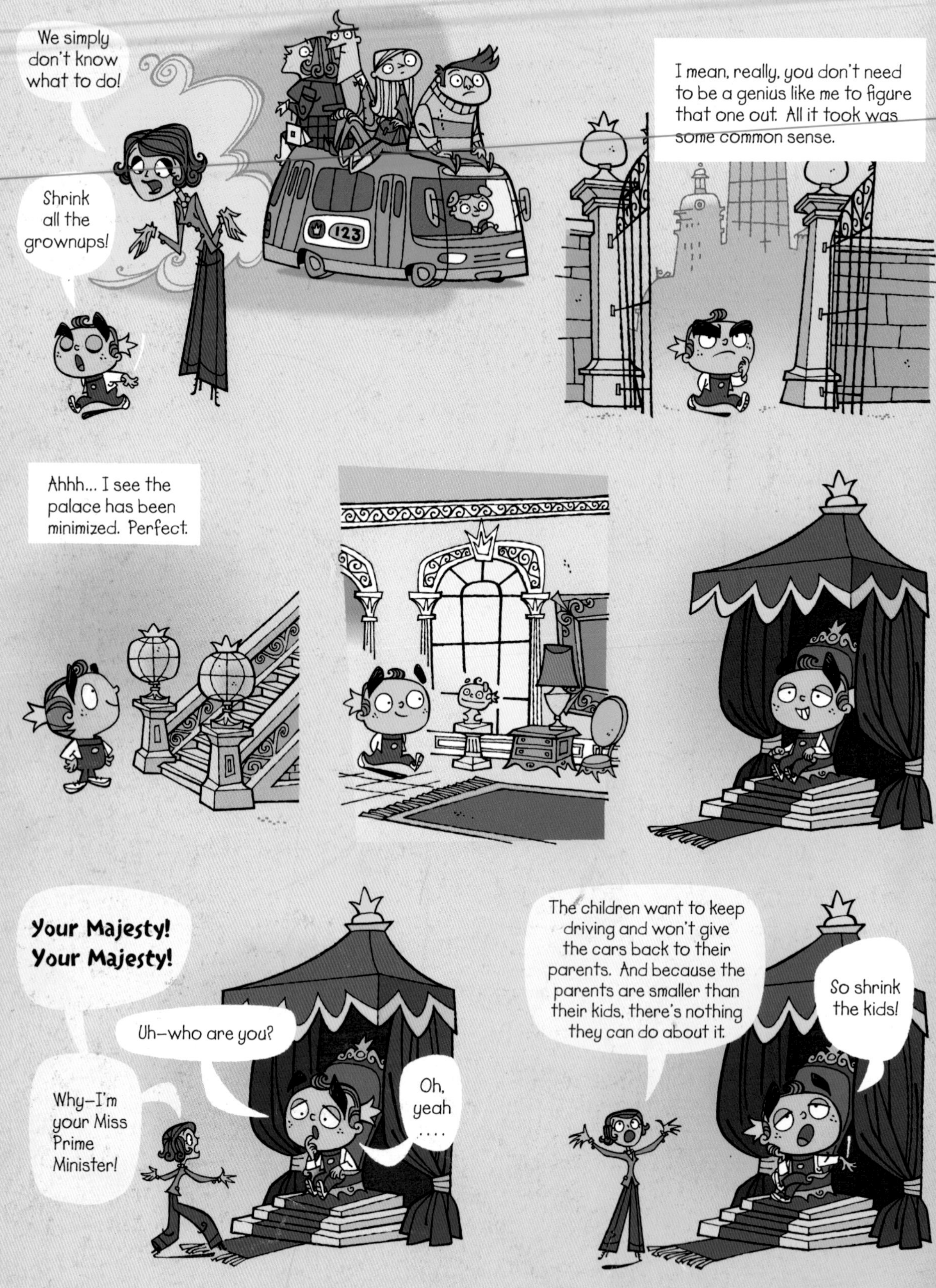
We simply don't know what to do!
Shrink all the grownups!
I mean, really, you don't need to be a genius like me to figure that one out. All it took was some common sense.
123
Ahhh... I see the palace has been minimized. Perfect.
Your Majesty! Your Majesty!
Uh—who are you?
Why—I'm your Miss Prime Minister!
Oh, yeah . . . .
The children want to keep driving and won't give the cars back to their parents. And because the parents are smaller than their kids, there's nothing they can do about it.
So shrink the kids!

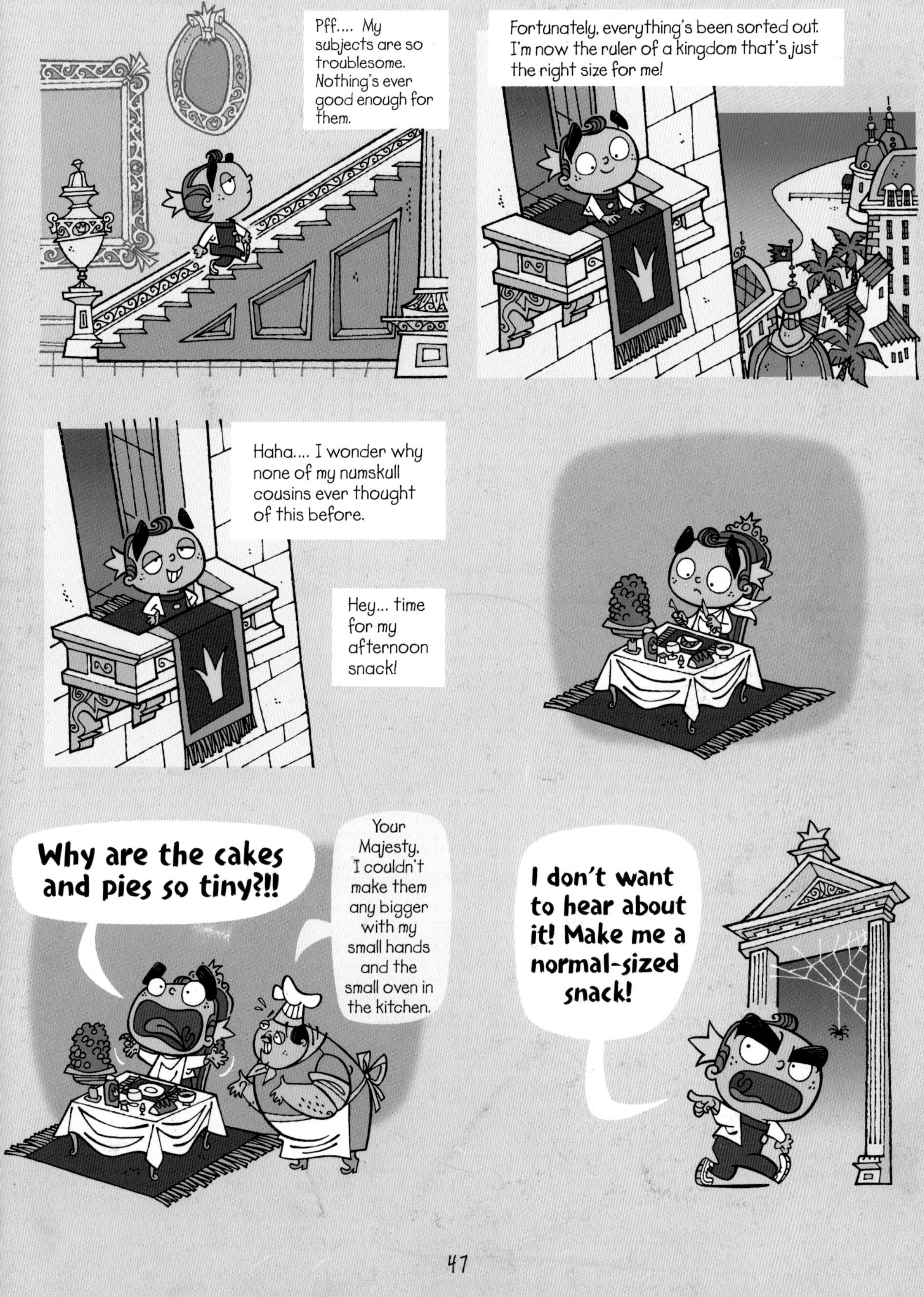
Pff.... My subjects are so troublesome. Nothing's ever good enough for them.
Fortunately, everything's been sorted out. I'm now the ruler of a kingdom that's just the right size for me!
Haha.... I wonder why none of my numskull cousins ever thought of this before.
Hey... time for my afternoon snack!
Why are the cakes and pies so tiny?!!
Your Majesty, I couldn't make them any bigger with my small hands and the small oven in the kitchen.
I don't want to hear about it! Make me a normal-sized snack!

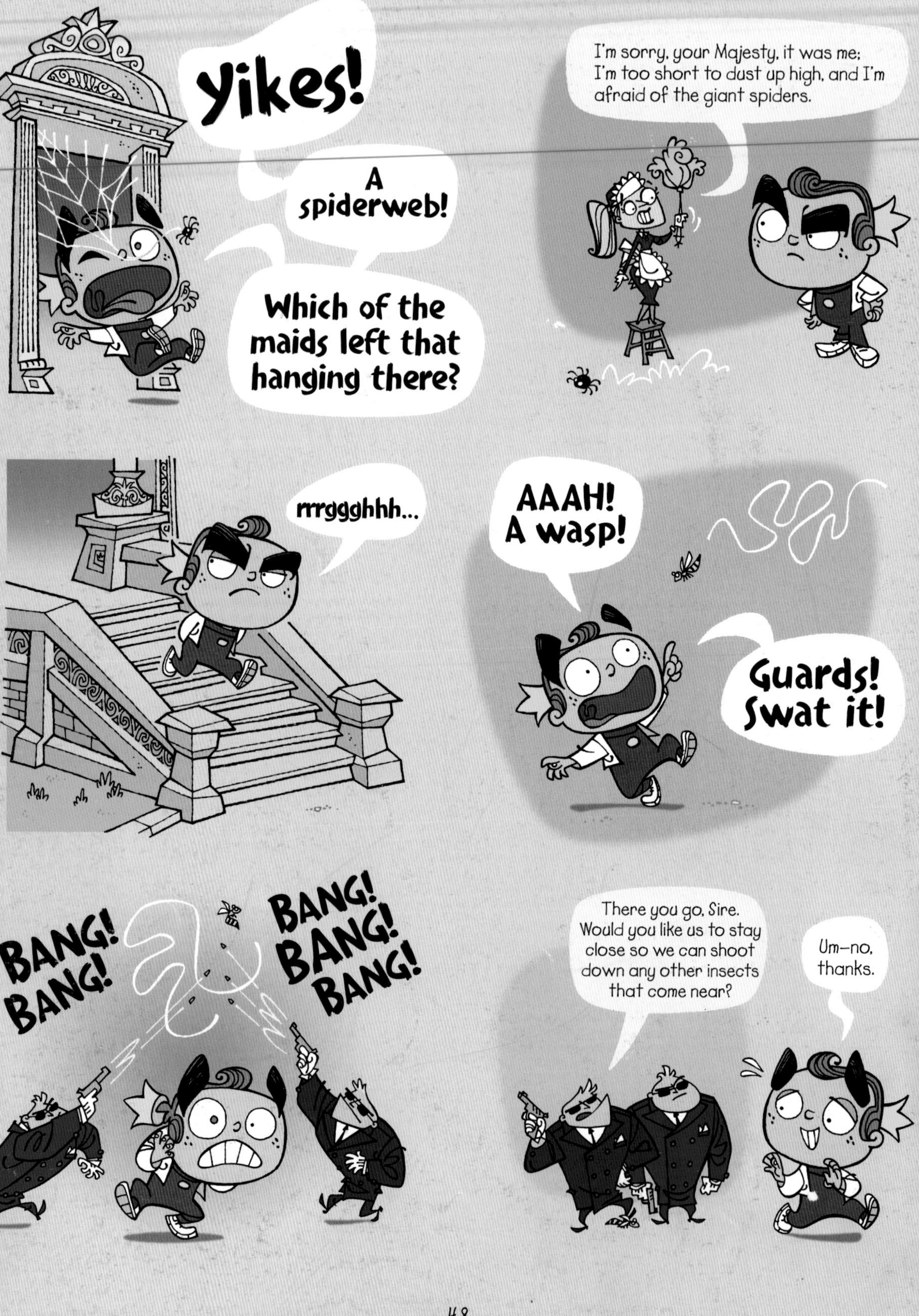
Yikes!
A spiderweb!
Which of the maids left that hanging there?
I'm sorry, your Majesty, it was me; I'm too short to dust up high, and I'm afraid of the giant spiders.
rrrggghhh...
AAAH! A wasp!
Guards! Swat it!
BANG! BANG!
BANG! BANG! BANG!
There you go, Sire. Would you like us to stay close so we can shoot down any other insects that come near?
Um—no, thanks.

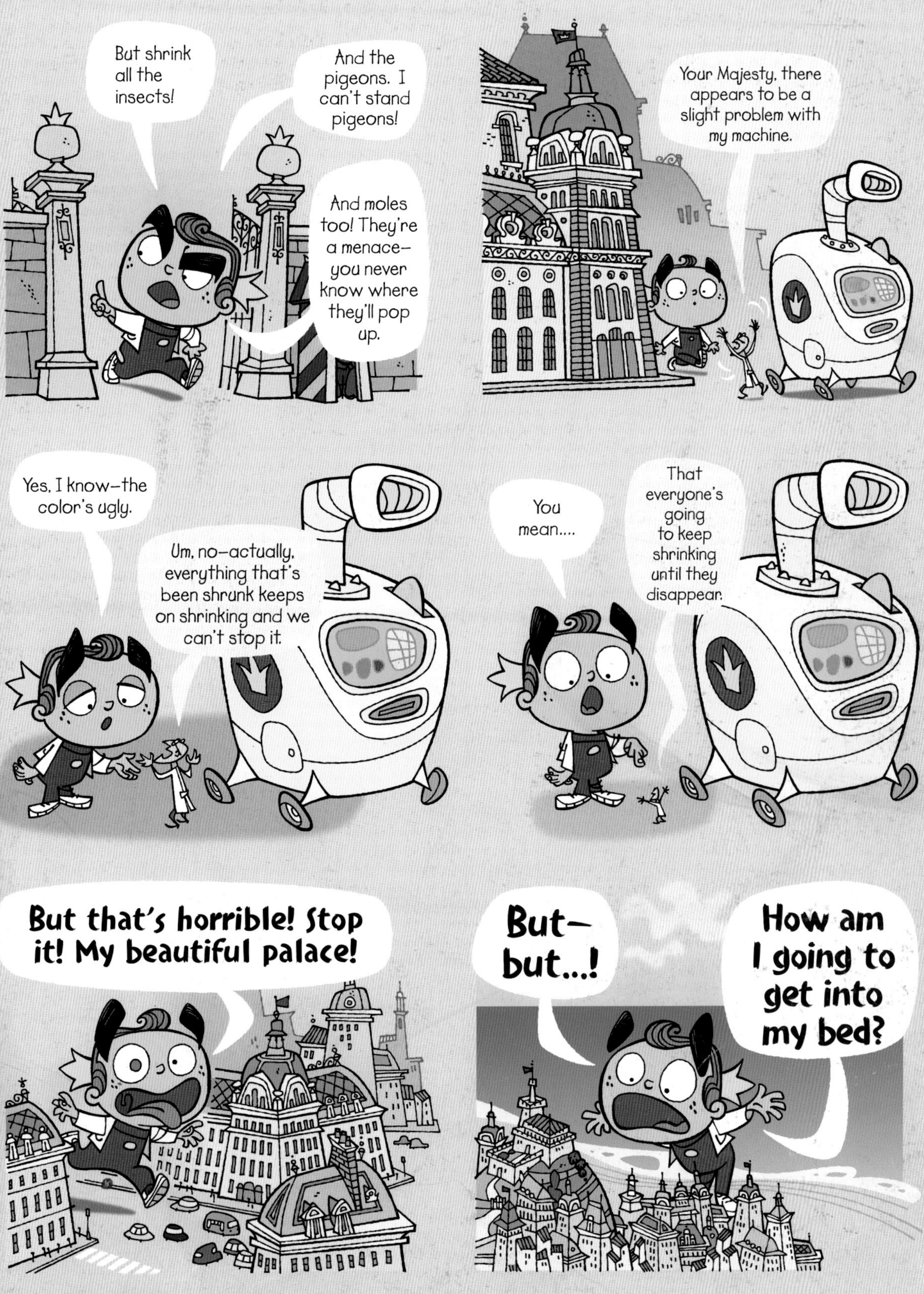

But shrink all the insects!
And the pigeons. I can't stand pigeons!
And moles too! They're a menace—you never know where they'll pop up.
Your Majesty, there appears to be a slight problem with my machine.
Yes, I know—the color's ugly.
Um, no—actually, everything that's been shrunk keeps on shrinking and we can't stop it.
You mean....
That everyone's going to keep shrinking until they disappear.
But that's horrible! Stop it! My beautiful palace!
But—but...!
How am I going to get into my bed?

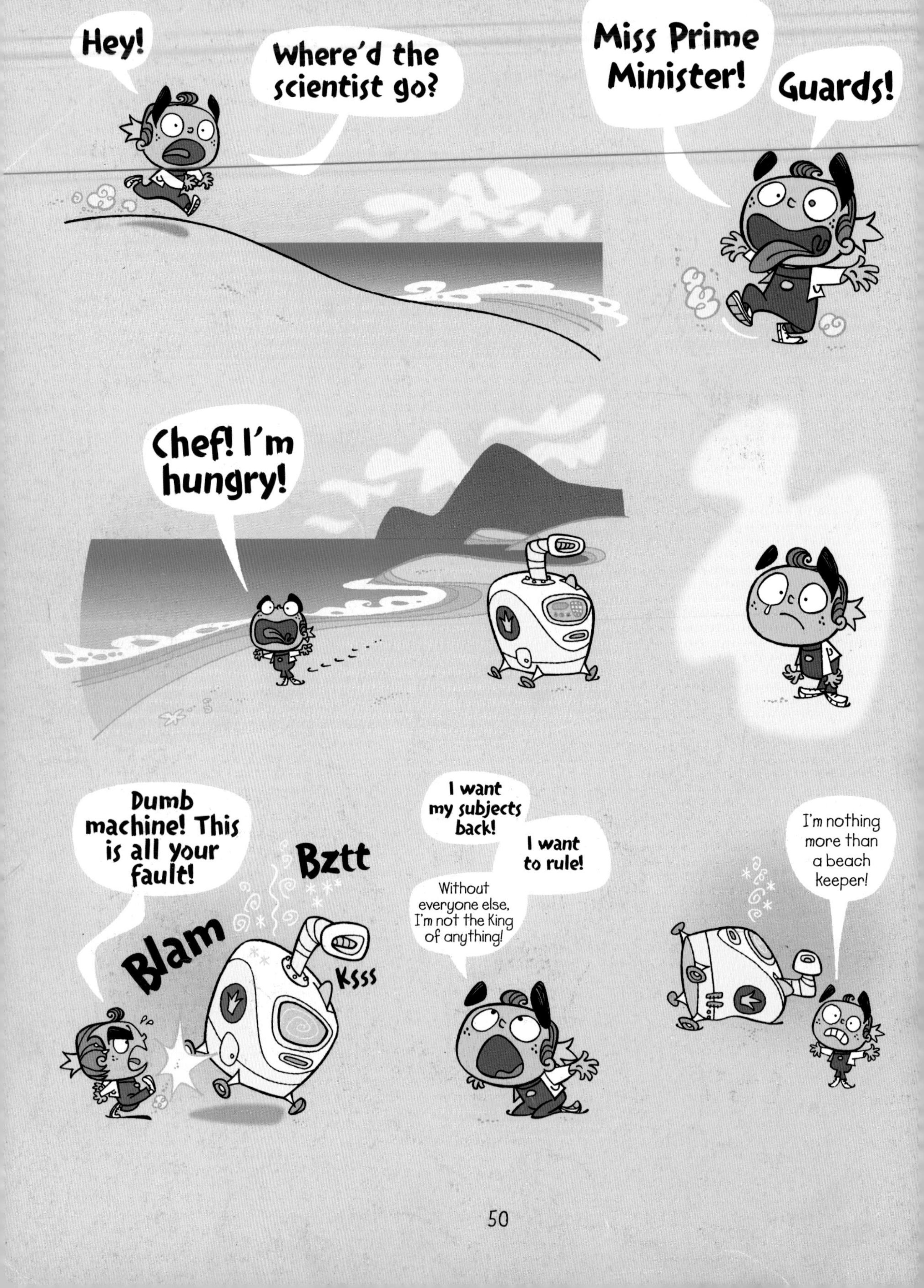
Hey!
Where'd the scientist go?
Miss Prime Minister!
Guards!
Chef! I'm hungry!
Dumb machine! This is all your fault!
Bztt
Blam
Ksss
I want my subjects back!
I want to rule!
Without everyone else, I'm not the King of anything!
I'm nothing more than a beach keeper!

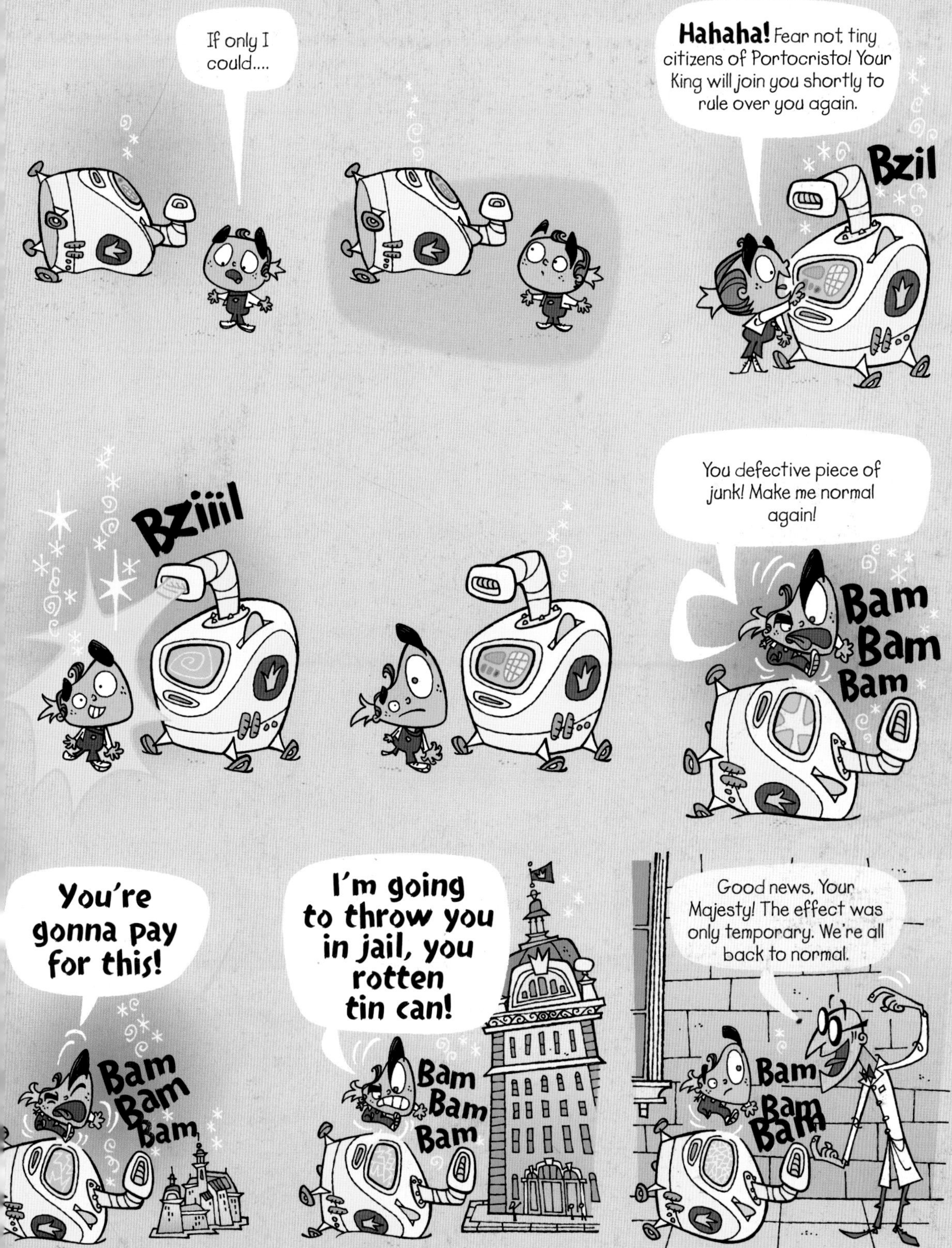
If only I could....
Hahaha! Fear not, tiny citizens of Portocristo! Your King will join you shortly to rule over you again.
Bzil
Bziiil
You defective piece of junk! Make me normal again!
Bam Bam Bam
You're gonna pay for this!
Bam Bam Bam
I'm going to throw you in jail, you rotten tin can!
Bam Bam Bam
Good news, Your Majesty! The effect was only temporary. We're all back to normal.
Bam Bam Bam

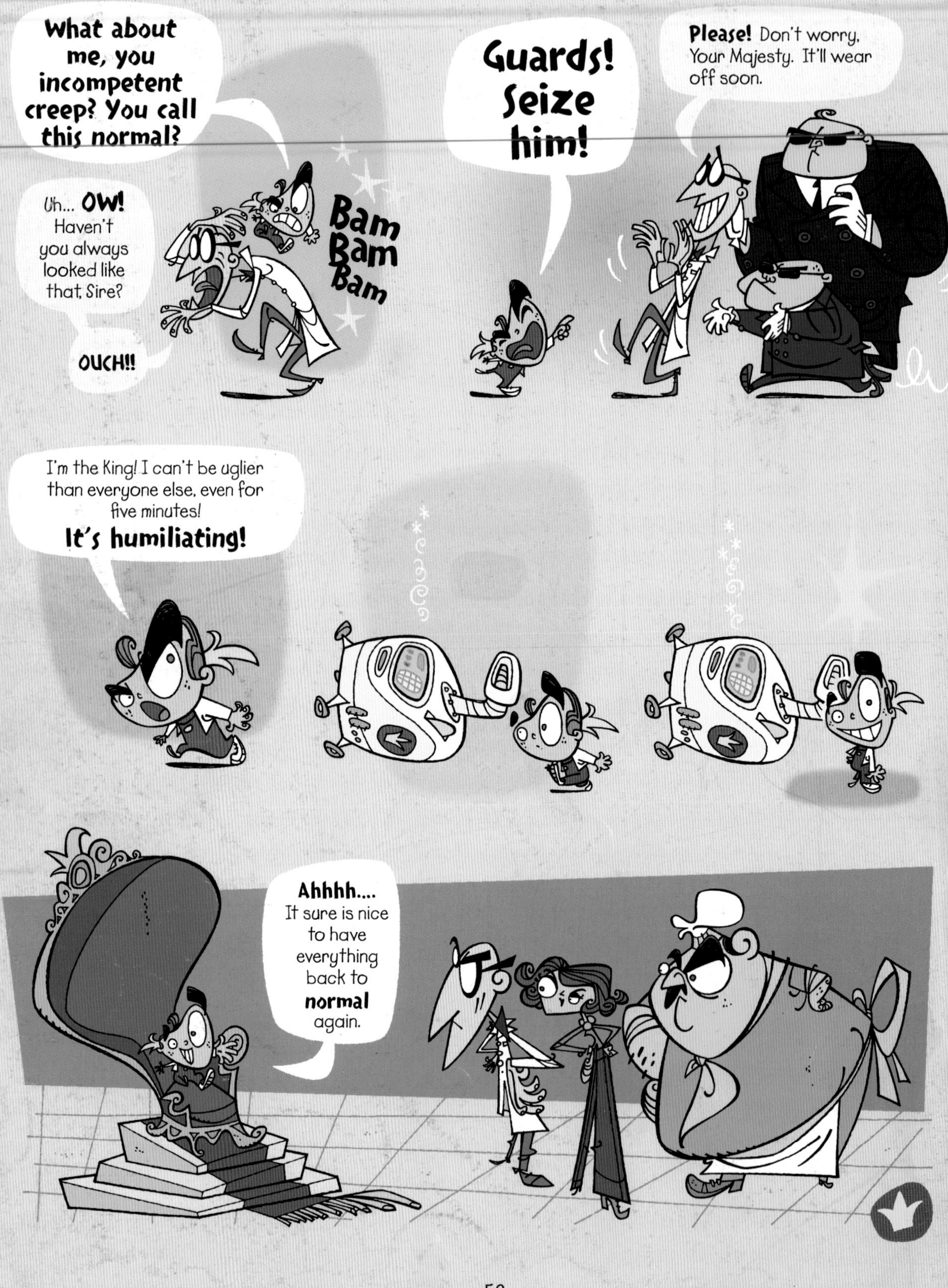

What about me, you incompetent creep? You call this normal?
Uh... OW! Haven't you always looked like that, Sire?
Bam Bam Bam
OUCH!!
Guards! Seize him!
Please! Don't worry, Your Majesty. It'll wear off soon.
I'm the King! I can't be uglier than everyone else, even for five minutes!
It's humiliating!
Ahhhh.... It sure is nice to have everything back to normal again.

A Full Life

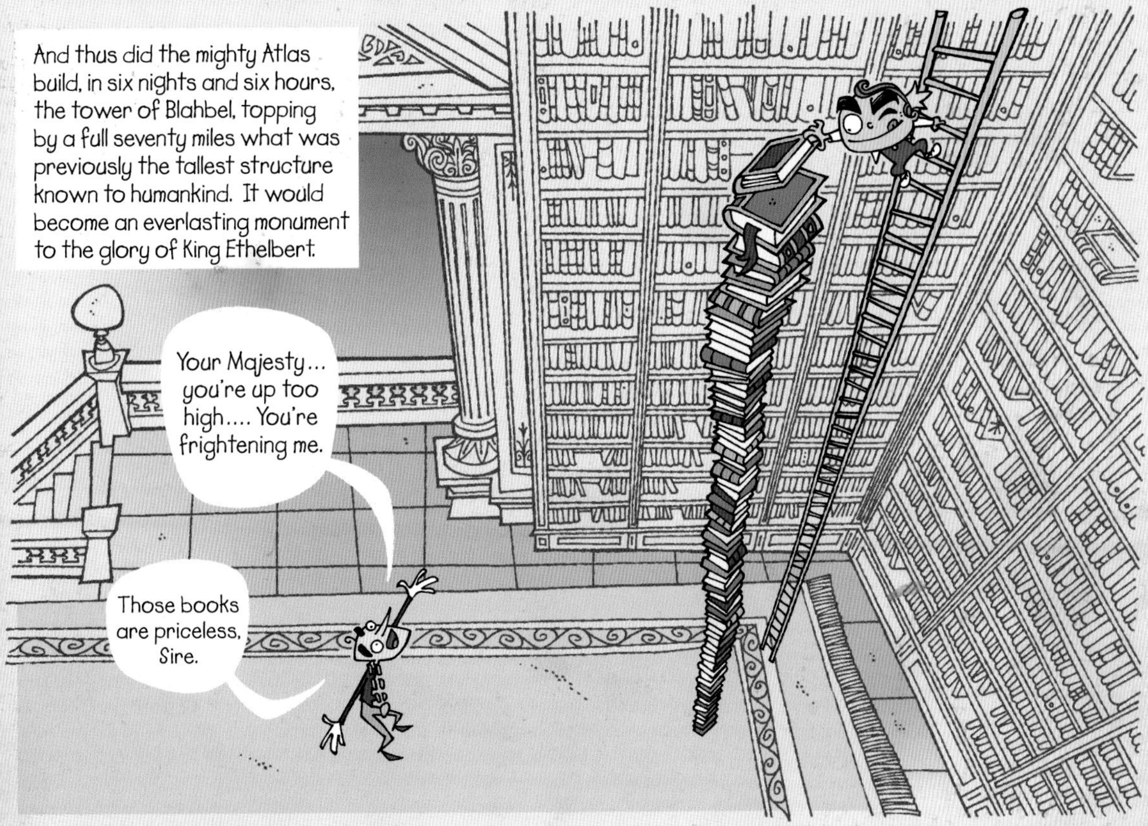
And thus did the mighty Atlas build, in six nights and six hours, the tower of Blahbel, topping by a full seventy miles what was previously the tallest structure known to humankind. It would become an everlasting monument to the glory of King Ethelbert.
Your Majesty... you're up too high.... You're frightening me.
Those books are priceless, Sire.

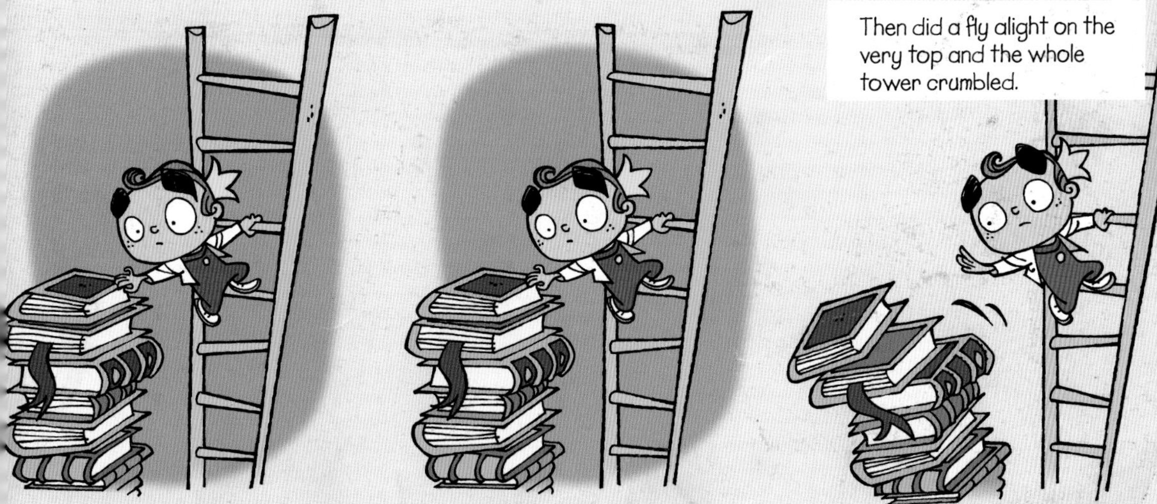
Then did a fly alight on the very top and the whole tower crumbled.

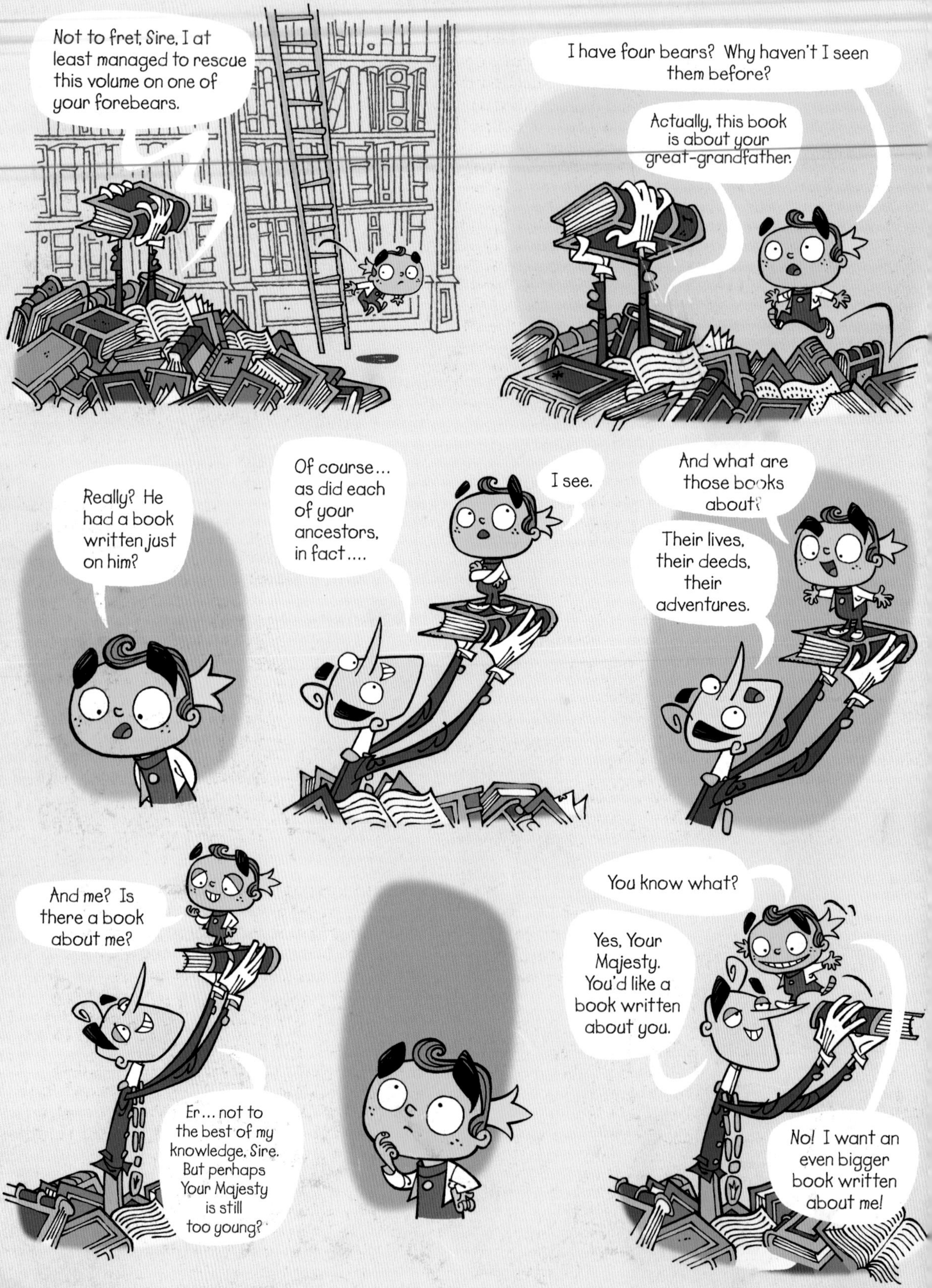
Not to fret, Sire, I at least managed to rescue this volume on one of your forebears.
I have four bears? Why haven't I seen them before?
Actually, this book is about your great-grandfather.
Really? He had a book written just on him?
Of course... as did each of your ancestors, in fact....
I see.
And what are those books about?
Their lives, their deeds, their adventures.
And me? Is there a book about me?
Er... not to the best of my knowledge, Sire. But perhaps Your Majesty is still too young?
You know what?
Yes, Your Majesty. You'd like a book written about you.
No! I want an even bigger book written about me!

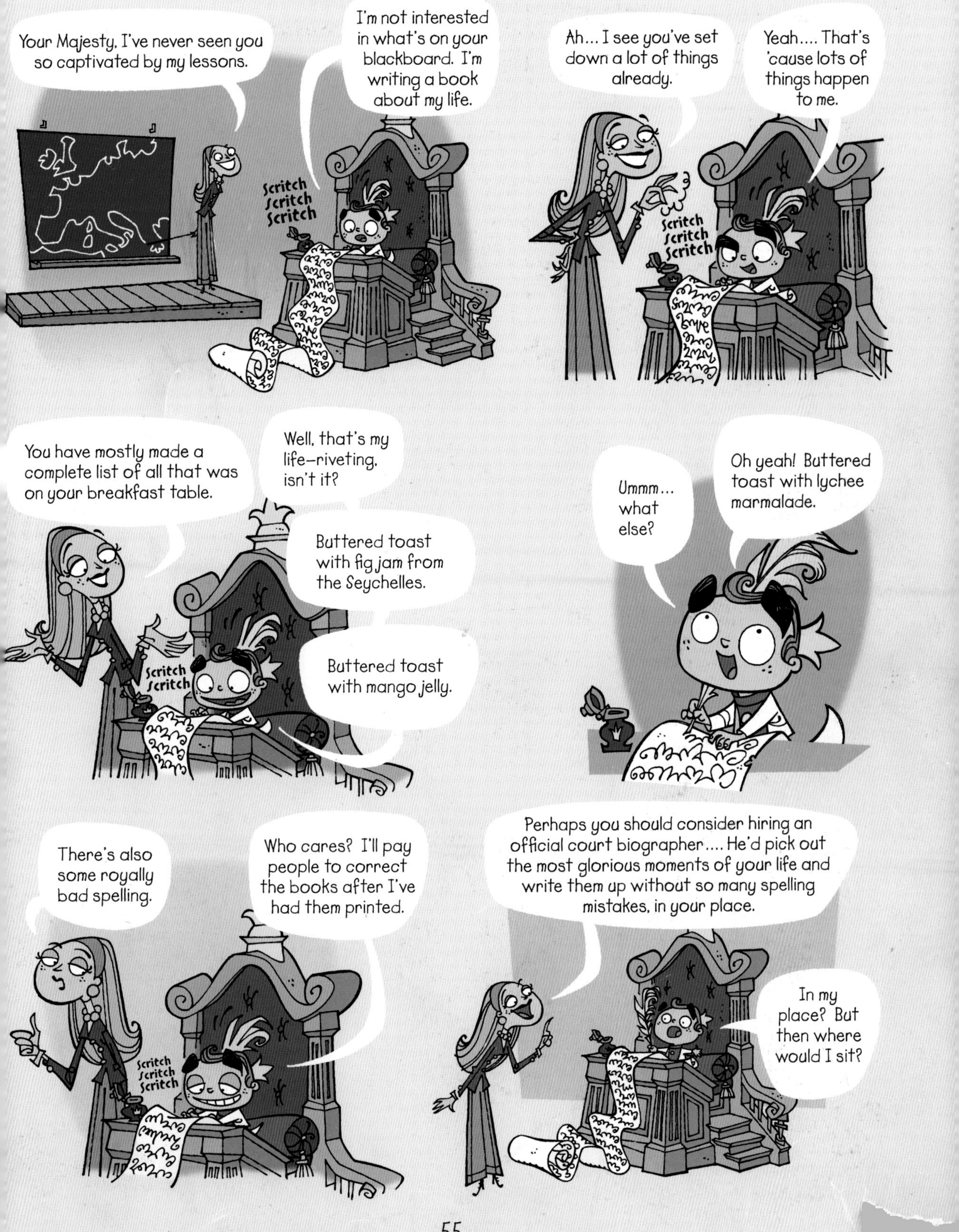
Your Majesty, I've never seen you so captivated by my lessons.
I'm not interested in what's on your blackboard. I'm writing a book about my life.
Scritch Scritch Scritch
Ah... I see you've set down a lot of things already.
Yeah.... That's 'cause lots of things happen to me.
Scritch Scritch Scritch
You have mostly made a complete list of all that was on your breakfast table.
Well, that's my life—riveting, isn't it?
Buttered toast with fig jam from the Seychelles.
Buttered toast with mango jelly.
Scritch Scritch
Ummm... what else?
Oh yeah! Buttered toast with lychee marmalade.
There's also some royally bad spelling.
Who cares? I'll pay people to correct the books after I've had them printed.
Scritch Scritch Scritch
Perhaps you should consider hiring an official court biographer.... He'd pick out the most glorious moments of your life and write them up without so many spelling mistakes, in your place.
In my place? But then where would I sit?

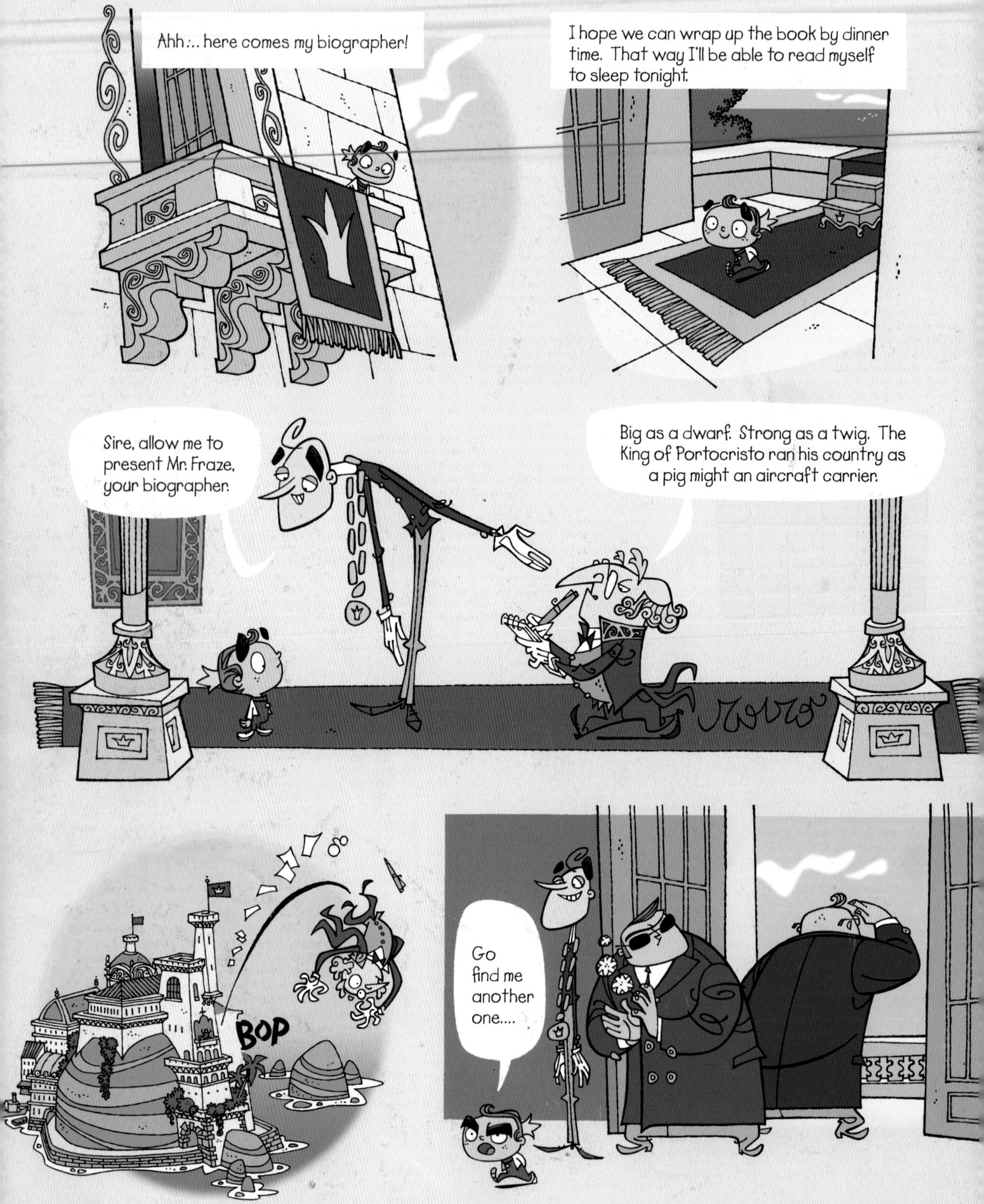
Ahh... here comes my biographer!
I hope we can wrap up the book by dinner time. That way I'll be able to read myself to sleep tonight.
Sire, allow me to present Mr. Fraze, your biographer.
Big as a dwarf. Strong as a twig. The King of Portocristo ran his country as a pig might an aircraft carrier.
BOP
Go find me another one....

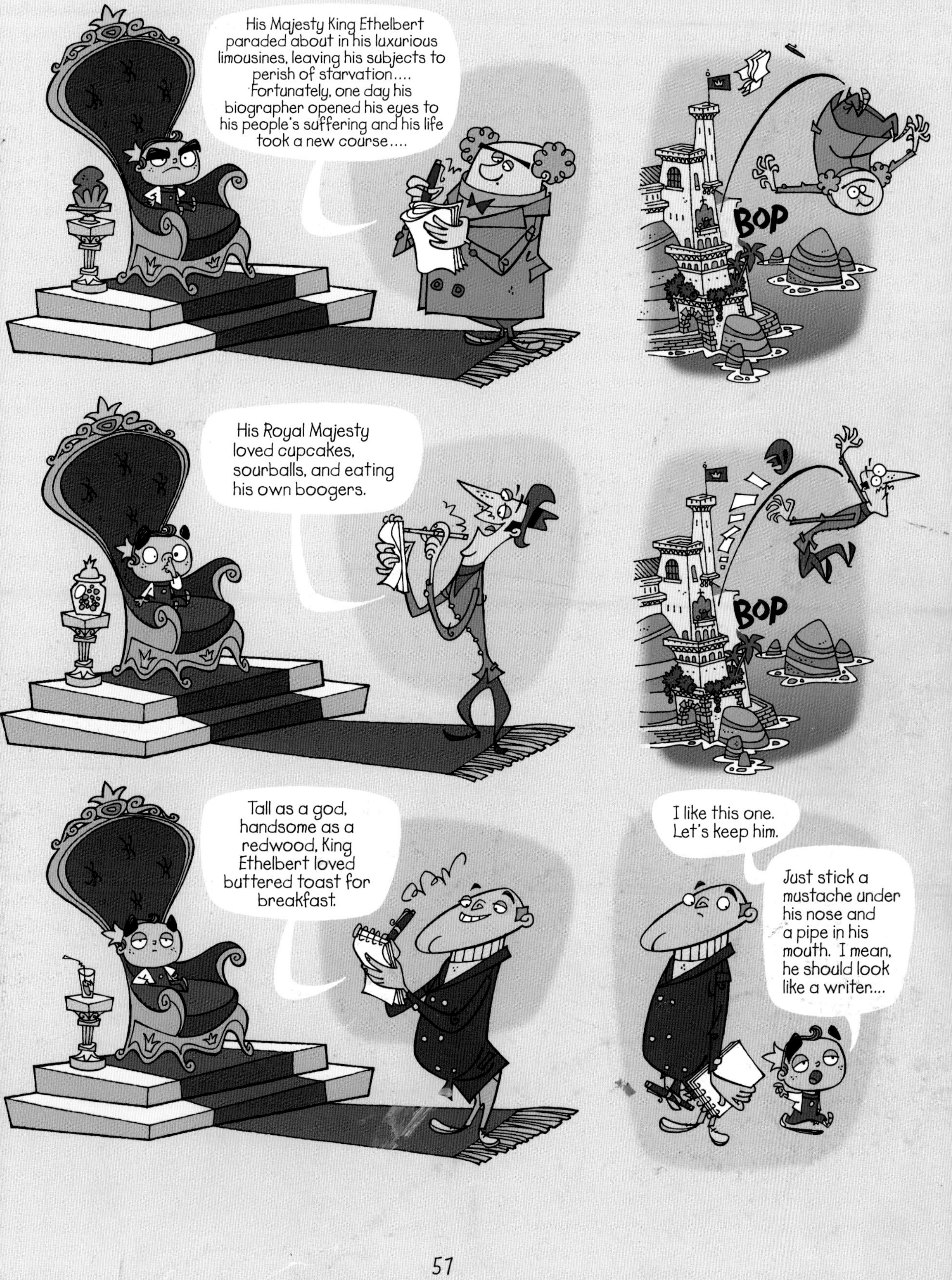
His Majesty King Ethelbert paraded about in his luxurious limousines, leaving his subjects to perish of starvation.... Fortunately, one day his biographer opened his eyes to his people's suffering and his life took a new course....
BOP
His *Royal* Majesty loved cupcakes, sourballs, and eating his own boogers.
BOP
Tall as a god, handsome as a redwood, King Ethelbert loved buttered toast for breakfast.
I like this one. Let's keep him.
Just stick a mustache under his nose and a pipe in his mouth. I mean, he should look like a writer...

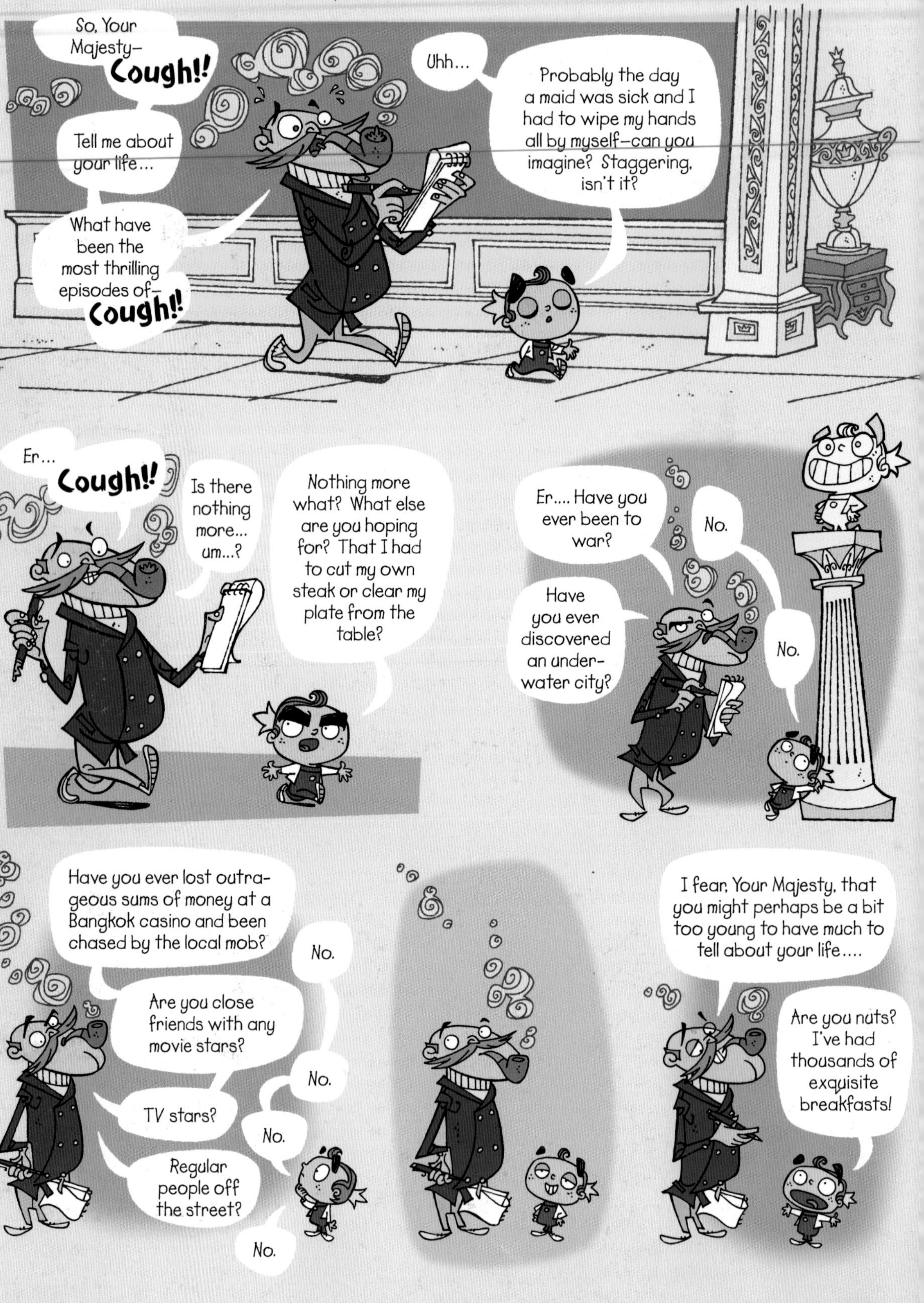
So, Your Majesty–
Cough!!
Tell me about your life...
What have been the most thrilling episodes of–
Cough!!
Uhh...
Probably the day a maid was sick and I had to wipe my hands all by myself—can you imagine? Staggering, isn't it?
Er...
Cough!!
Is there nothing more... um...?
Nothing more what? What else are you hoping for? That I had to cut my own steak or clear my plate from the table?
Er.... Have you ever been to war?
No.
Have you ever discovered an under-water city?
No.
Have you ever lost outra-geous sums of money at a Bangkok casino and been chased by the local mob?
No.
Are you close friends with any movie stars?
No.
TV stars?
No.
Regular people off the street?
No.
I fear, Your Majesty, that you might perhaps be a bit too young to have much to tell about your life....
Are you nuts? I've had thousands of exquisite breakfasts!

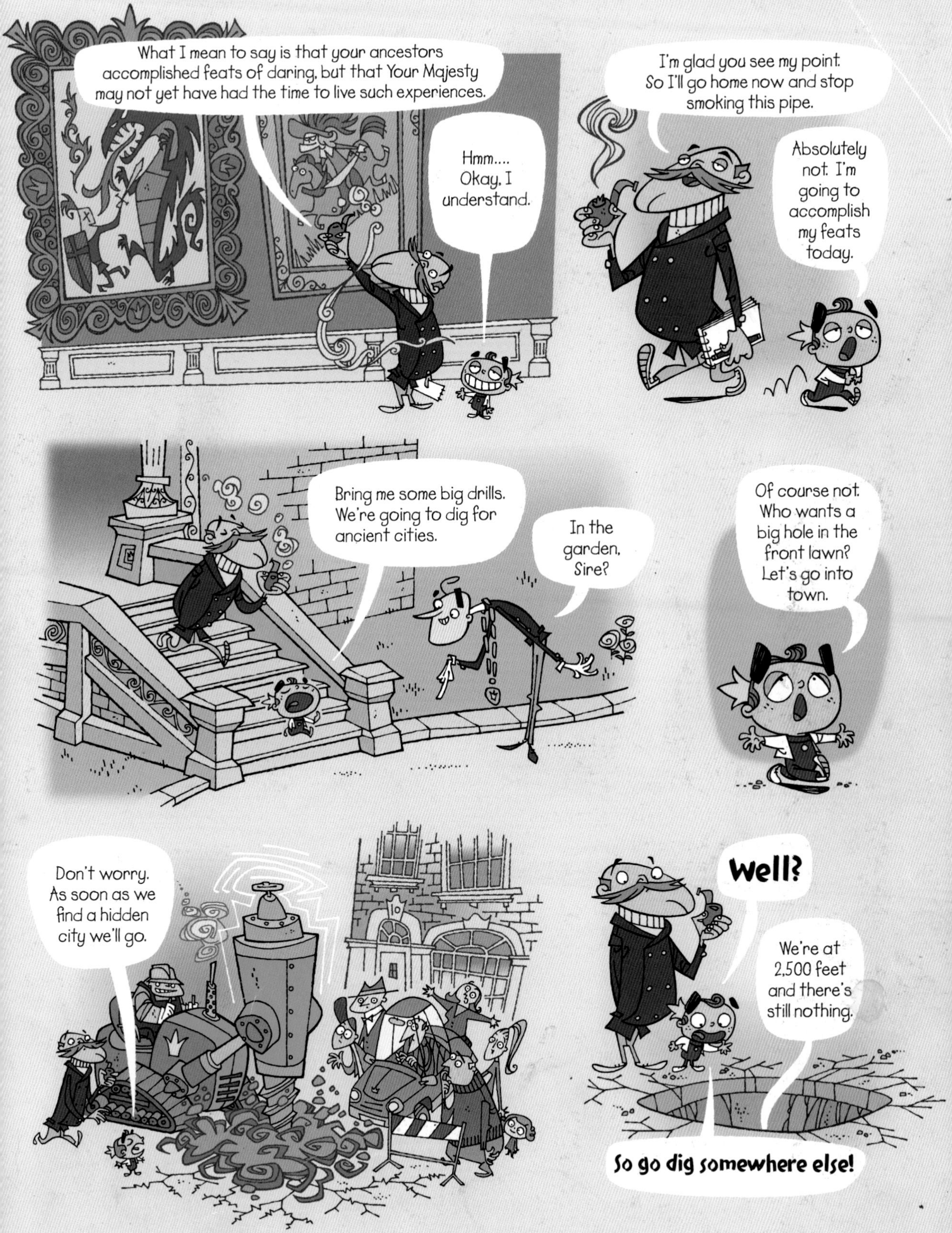
What I mean to say is that your ancestors accomplished feats of daring, but that Your Majesty may not yet have had the time to live such experiences.
Hmm.... Okay, I understand.
I'm glad you see my point. So I'll go home now and stop smoking this pipe.
Absolutely not. I'm going to accomplish my feats today.
Bring me some big drills. We're going to dig for ancient cities.
In the garden, Sire?
Of course not. Who wants a big hole in the front lawn? Let's go into town.
Don't worry. As soon as we find a hidden city we'll go.
Well?
We're at 2,500 feet and there's still nothing.
So go dig somewhere else!

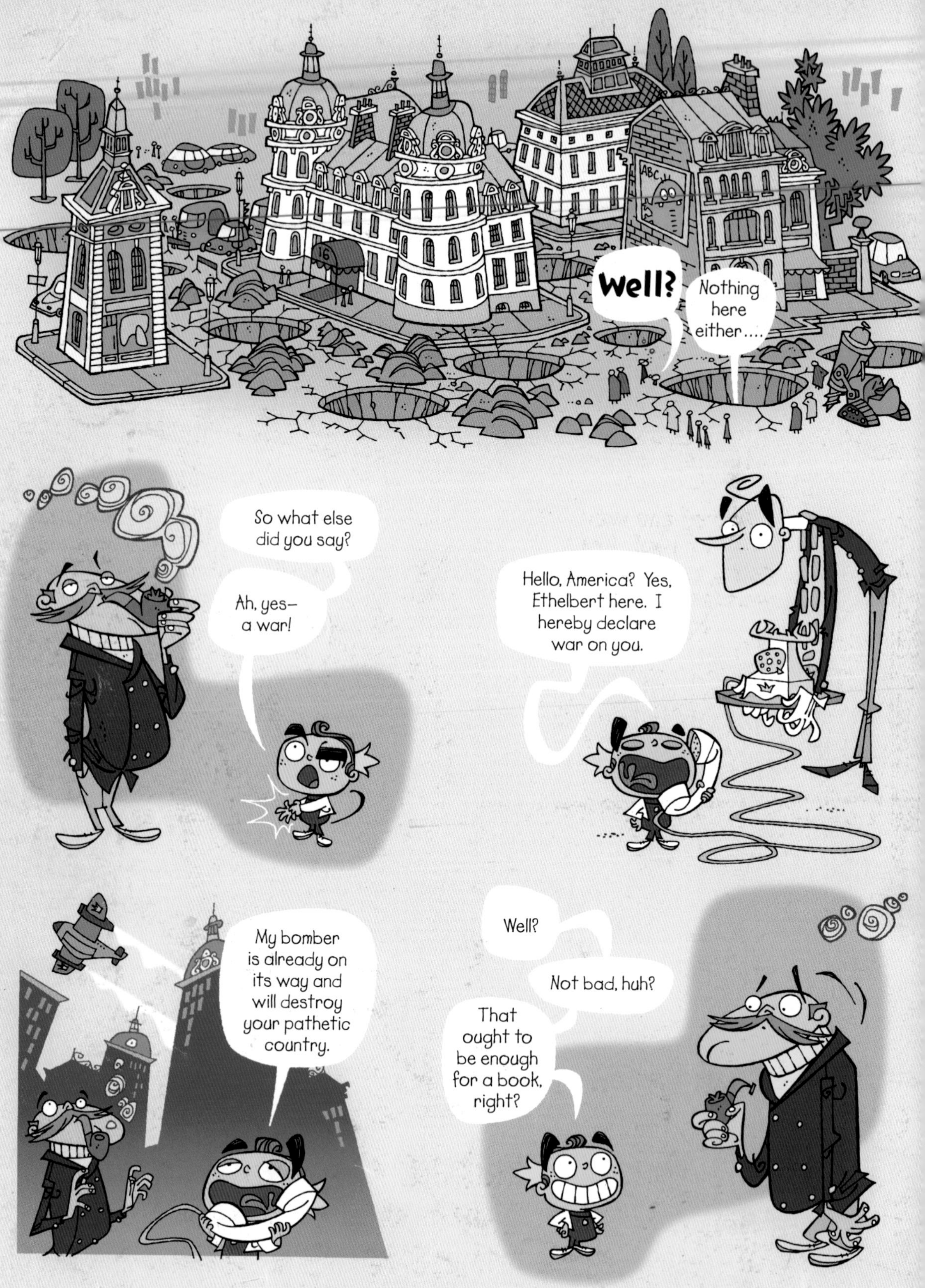
Well?
Nothing here either....
So what else did you say?
Ah, yes— a war!
Hello, America? Yes, Ethelbert here. I hereby declare war on you.
My bomber is already on its way and will destroy your pathetic country.
Well?
Not bad, huh?
That ought to be enough for a book, right?

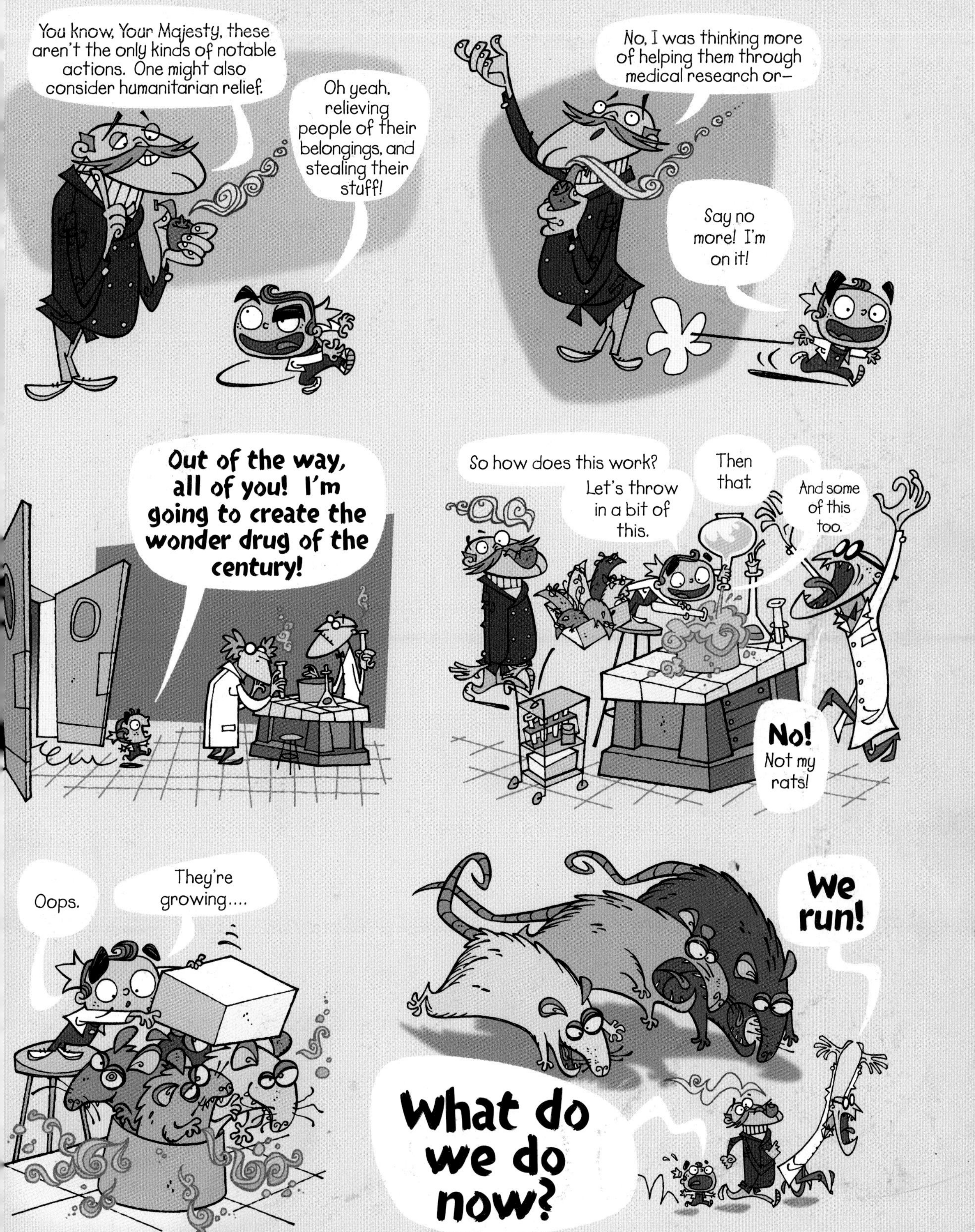
You know, Your Majesty, these aren't the only kinds of notable actions. One might also consider humanitarian relief.
Oh yeah, relieving people of their belongings, and stealing their stuff!
No, I was thinking more of helping them through medical research or—
Say no more! I'm on it!
Out of the way, all of you! I'm going to create the wonder drug of the century!
So how does this work?
Let's throw in a bit of this.
Then that.
And some of this too.
No! Not my rats!
Oops.
They're growing....
We run!
What do we do now?

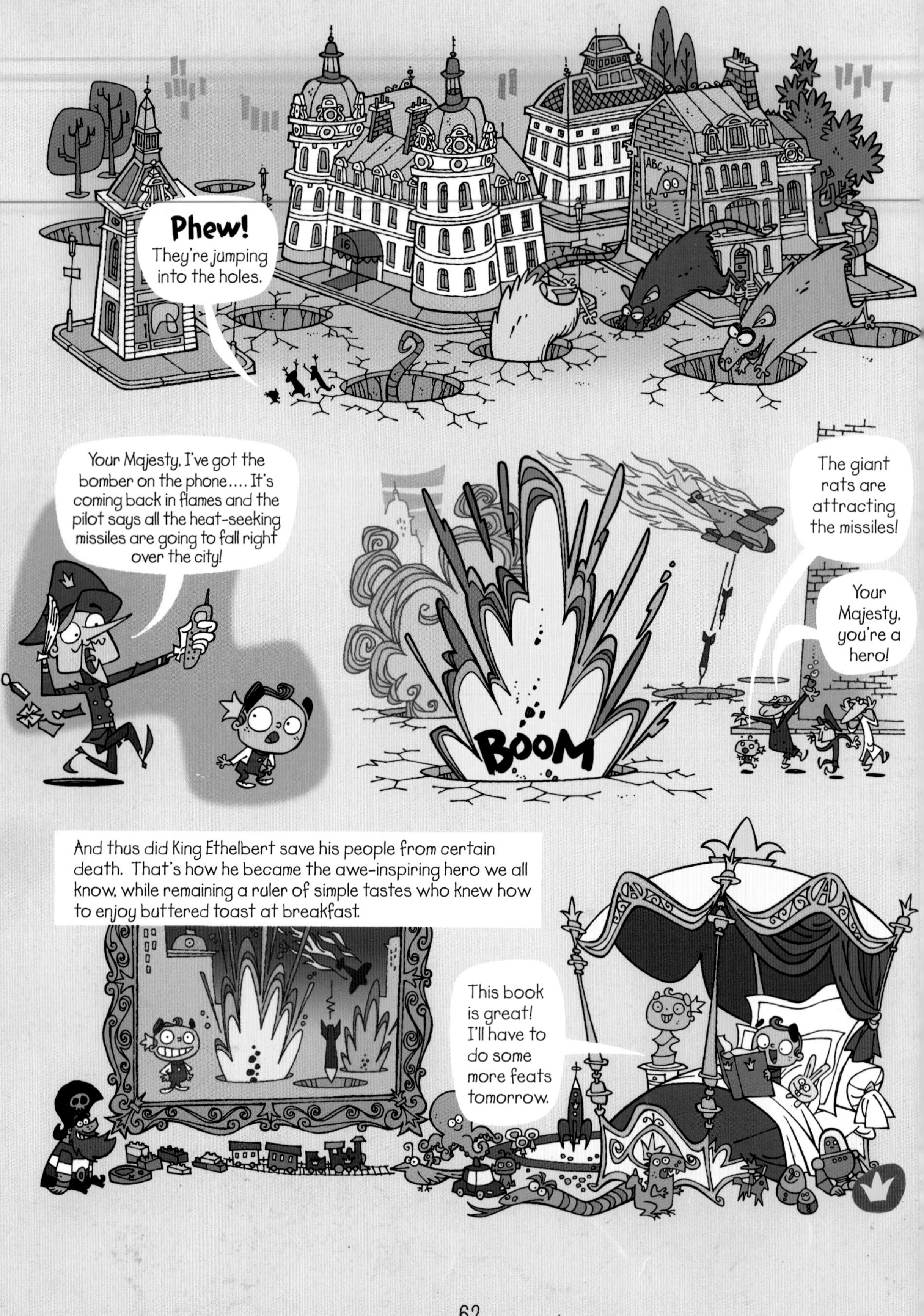
Phew! They're jumping into the holes.
Your Majesty, I've got the bomber on the phone.... It's coming back in flames and the pilot says all the heat-seeking missiles are going to fall right over the city!
BOOM
The giant rats are attracting the missiles!
Your Majesty, you're a hero!
And thus did King Ethelbert save his people from certain death. That's how he became the awe-inspiring hero we all know, while remaining a ruler of simple tastes who knew how to enjoy buttered toast at breakfast.
This book is great! I'll have to do some more feats tomorrow.

If you liked
this book,
tell a friend!

If you
didn't, tell
an enemy!

First Second

New York & London

Copyright © 2001, 2002, 2003, 2004 by Guy Delcourt Productions—
Lewis Trondheim—Fabrice Parme
English translation copyright © 2007 by First Second

Published by First Second
First Second is an imprint of Roaring Brook Press,
a division of Holtzbrinck Publishing Holdings Limited Partnership
175 Fifth Avenue, New York, NY 10010

Distributed in Canada by H. B. Fenn and Company Ltd.
Distributed in the United Kingdom by Macmillan Children's Books, a division of Pan Macmillan.

Originally published in France in 2001 under the title *Adalbert ne manqué pas d'air,* in 2002 under the title *Adalbert a tout pour plaire,* in 2003 under the title *Adalbert fait du scandale,* in 2004 under the title *Adalbert change d'atmosphère* by Guy Delcourt Productions, Paris.

Design by Tanja Geis and Danica Novgorodoff

Colored by Fabrice Parme and Véronique Dreher

Cataloging-in-Publication Data is on file at the Library of Congress.

ISBN-13: 978-1-59643-523-0
ISBN-10: 1-59643-523-2

First Second books are available for special promotions and premiums.
For details, contact: Director of Special Markets, Holtzbrinck Publishers.

First American Edition April 2007

Printed in May 2009 in China by South China Printing Co. Ltd., Dongguan City, Guangdong Province

1 3 5 7 9 10 8 6 4 2